An Anthology Curated by

Ishika Jain

Inkfeathers Publishing
www.inkfeathers.com

Days to Relive
Edited & Compiled by Ishika Jain
Paperback Edition

First Published in India in 2023 by
Inkfeathers Publishing
New Delhi 110095

ISBN 978-93-90882-77-9



www.inkfeathers.com

*Featuring the writings of*

Deepika Kumari, Tiyasa Tikadar, Mouly Dangarwala, Katyani Sharma, Rashmita Nayak, Jasmeen Bagga, Halo C, Ananya Duggal, Sakshi Khillare, Namrata Prajapati, S.R. Behera, Priyanka Reddy, Juveriya Bilal, Mitali Kushwaha, Harleen Kaur, Kriti Mohanty, Kumud Jain, Dhruv Kataria, Huda Nadeem, Krish Malhotra, Ananya Barman, Anwesha Banerjee, Arjun Unnikrishnan, Yashvi Bulani, Jash Chauhan, Dhriti Mehra, Ishika Jain

*Disclaimer*

The anthology “Days to Relive” is a collection of 21 poems and 14 stories written by 26 authors who belong to different parts of the world.

Unless otherwise indicated, all the names, characters, objects, businesses, places, events, incidents—whether physical/non-physical, real/unreal, tangible/ intangible in whatsoever description used in this book are either the product of the author’s imagination or used in a fictitious manner. Any resemblance to actual persons, objects, entities, living or dead, or actual events is purely coincidental.

The contents published in this book are solely owned by their respective authors and are in no way intended to hurt anyone’s religious, political, spiritual, brand, personal or fanatic beliefs and/or faith, whatsoever. In case, any sort of plagiarism is detected in the contents within this anthology or in case of any complaints, grievances, or objections, neither the anthology editor nor the publisher is to be held responsible.

For me,

For you,

And for everyone who's out there
wanting to relive their school days.

Stay young at heart, always.

# Contents

# Meet the Editor

**Ishika Jain** is an ardent reader and writer, who ventured into the world of books at a young age and hasn't been able to escape it since. Hoping to pursue journalism as a career, she is also a successfully published author. Her debut YA novel titled "17 Days and Die" was traditionally published in early 2022 and has received absolute love and adoration from her readers. She has also managed to enter the India Book of Records. She has also participated in many anthologies, and this is her first time editing one. She hopes to change lives with her writing and stories.

She can be reached on Instagram @ishikasbookshelf.

# Editor's Note

Someone I really look up to said this once: *every place you've ever been will never be the same, and neither will you.*

I realise, not everyone's had the best high school experiences. Some of you had it worse than others and may not want to look back at those times. The intention to publish this anthology was to make you feel good about those little happy moments that overshadowed the bad ones. Those experiences which made passing through school just a little bit easier. The day you found your best friend while you were busy coping with your first breakup? Wouldn't you want to relive that day just once more to mend your dwindling friendship now and remind yourself how lucky you are to be their friend?

And for those who had a delight, like me, this anthology is all about making you happy and making you call the friends you promised to stay in contact with but haven't yet texted more than five times.

High school has always been a special place for me. Not to toot my own horn at all, but I don't think there was any co-curricular activity that I hadn't participated in or any extra club I wasn't a part of. But then, COVID struck, and I lost my junior and senior year along the way. I think somewhere in 2020, I got so used to staying at home that the mere thought of schools reopening made me break out in sweat. And then my senior year began in March 2021, and honestly, going to school was such a chore because let's face it, all of us went through the lockdown lounging on our beds and binge-watching Netflix. So, to leave all that comfort and return to school to study? God, I hated the mere idea of it. I remember going out to lunch with a friend and both of us just reminiscing about our school's Christmas celebrations, and that was the exact moment the pitch for this anthology came to mind. One second, I was laughing and telling my friend about all of my classmates teasing me about my obsession with Harry Styles during Christmas inter-class competitions, and the next, I was gushing about this great idea for a book.

I've built so many friendships, so many relationships, loved so many teachers and absolutely enjoyed the hell out of my high school years. I've always known I wanted to compile and edit my own anthology one day, given that I'd participated in many and worked under glorious writers and editors. And I knew, this theme was something that would hit home for so many people.

High school experiences are something that I don't think anyone is ever going to get over. The breakups, the fights, the laughter, the punishments, the bunks… it was such a youthful time for all of us, and honestly, all I wish to happen with the release of this anthology is to give an ode to that essence of childishness in all of us.

I sincerely hope the stories and poems in this anthology, some of which include topics considered taboo by our society but not limited to them, will compel you to just look back fondly to your school days and ignite that spark of happiness and playfulness in your busy lives. I had so much fun editing and compiling these stories, and I hope you'll love reading them, too.

# Acknowledgments

This anthology holds a very special place in my heart, especially since 2022 was my last high school academic year, and the journey was such a bittersweet experience that words won't be able to do it justice.

This anthology wouldn't have been possible without my parents. My dad, Yatin Jain, who kept encouraging me to complete this anthology no matter what and my mum, Harsha Jain, who patiently sat through all of my ramblings about everyone's stories. My grandparents, who never once failed to keep up with all the extended deadlines and updates.

And of course, all of the writers who participated in this anthology: guys, you did it! This anthology wouldn't have come this far without you all jumping in to save the day with your absolutely enchanting stories and poems. I love every single one of you and it's been one hell of a ride.

To my closest friends—Mouly, Katyani, Jasmeen, Tiyasa, Rashmita, Kumud, Krish... thank you so much for joining in on this anthology. It was an absolute freaking delight working with you all.

Thank you to Inkfeathers Publishing who considered my idea worthy enough to be published as an anthology.

And to everyone out there who counted on me, who counted on us... this book is for you!

1.

# The Golden Era

Deepika Kumari

*Trinngggg.....trinngggg....*

*'Ek pen de na* (Can I have a pen, please?)'

*'Arre yaar aaj fir se boring chemical experiments!* (Urgh, we've got those boring chemical experiments again!)'

*'Yaar...achaar ki khushboo aa rahi kya kisi ko?* (Is anyone else smelling pickles too?)'

*'Wo dekh, Rahul ki crush jaa rahi...Raaahuuul...* (Look! It's Rahul's crush… Raaahuuul…)'

And Rahul's cheeks turned the shade of a tomato.

Did anything strike in that head of yours after listening to this phone-like sound, and those silly talks?

Yes, it was the sound of "freedom", and general talks of high school students, and without these talks, their food never got digested; a sound which was an order to run through the ground and corridors; a sound which silently said, 'Just run, create memories, you are going to miss these times a few decades later'; a sound in which our dearest teacher entered, a sound which made our feet and hands go cold because, *'humne assignment to kar li hai, par copy ghar par chhut gyi hai* (we've completed the assignment but we forgot the notebook at home).'

*Oh man, those excuses!*

Whenever, we, the high school retired ones listen to this *tringgg...trinnggg,* even today, a blast of memories takes place in which entire high school's fun-filled tragedies, happenings and tantrums run through our minds all at once. The way we used to go to school in neat and tidy uniforms yet return from school in charcoal blacks. This sound strikes a feeling of nostalgia about how innocent we used to be; about our activities, our corporate meetings for Teacher's Day; single tiffin boxes and mangled hands; a world war for a piece of mango pickle; that Grand Assembly Hall and most importantly the first and fresh air of love.

Yes, it's our dearest Middle and High School memories which gave us a lot of tickling memories and experiences which will be clinging with us for eternity.

High School is that "potter", who has shaped its "clay" with firmness and strictness to be a better and strong "vessel" of tomorrow.

Most importantly, high school has gifted us with "Sea of Memories", whose tides are still agile in heart.

So, what are you waiting for? Just tighten your seat belts and let's ride in the rocket of memories which will take you to the "space" of high school. Just consider this page as "anywhere door", and it will take you to the carefree, good, old days!

High School is a land where we come to learn about crucial aspects of life, while having nonstop fun. At first, most of us were nervous due to the new teachers, we were going to meet, whether they will be grumpy, red-faced or polite enough. Whether the classmates will be bullied? What if they will be cruel, or will they be sweet pies? Numerous confusions were jamming in the head. A common question, we all have questioned with ourselves: 'Will High school be same as elementary classes?' Because in elementary sections, our parents helped us in our homework and diary signings, to our school uniforms and bag packing.

But in High school, we had our mature projects, viva-voice, educational events, labs and what not.

We had to make certain decisions on our own, such as Olympiad participation, giving our names to school trips on the last day, on our own. So in total, High school was a completely different experience in context of higher studies and certain life making decisions.

Those who have attended their high school must prove the people wrong, who say, 'High school is only about higher studies, burden of notes and loads of projects and assignments.' But in my opinion, 'Yes, it's full of scientific and practical studies, but, at the same time, it's full of craziness, excitement and fun. It's full of strict and sweet teachers, buddies, right-left of P.T. to the smash of badminton.'

Overall, it's a full package gift that we receive in our entire life. And for us, "those days" are just unforgettable and precious of all. We had a life of fun, excitement and joy during those four years. Fun like, we allied with our classmates to plan some crazy activities and that evil plan was executed so precisely, that nobody would get a glimpse, unless and until, it was revealed by that "plan spoiler". It was the daily routine of ours, to be a nuisance in class in the absence of teacher.

High school was full of new experiences, new projects and new responsibilities. We spent a quite long time with our classmates, doing fun-filled activities.

Have you ever experienced a deep sleep during the most monotonous lecture, just after the lunch? Yes, I've experienced that, so I can share mine. Being the class president, I was assigned first bench as my permanent seat. It was really difficult even to put our head down, during the lecture of that grumpy sir. And he taught us in such a way, as he was singing a cradle song. That was just irresistible and sweet sleep of midday. I just kept my eyes wide open, but my brain was taking a sweet nap. And when there was a disturbance or any sharp voice, a quick awake of brain took place. 'Yes…feeling fresher' (brain conveyed) … Water bottle always helped us to be awake during those tedious lectures.

How can we forget those tiffins? No, no…Not in recess, but in between the lectures, just before the lunch period and at the back seat, so that '*khaa ke thora aaram bhi kar sake* (so that we could rest after we ate)'. Chemistry teacher was explaining, what to mix with HcL to give froth: Acid or base? And at the last bench, it was another chemistry brewing that, what to mix with sandwich to make it more rich; chilli sauce or tomato ketchup?... while someone was confused, what to eat with potato fries: puri or paratha? That strong and spicy aroma of '*Aam ka Achaar* (mango pickle)' kept power, even to distract the teacher.

Being the first bencher, I was never indulged in back seat lunch programs, but I was a devil, a plan spoiler. Whenever the aroma of any eatable tickled my olfactory elements, I interrupted, 'Excuse me sir, is somebody having their lunch?'…Sometimes, I was given the bribe of LAYS, just to keep my mouth sealed. 'Just keep your mouth shut, 50% of the total content will be yours.'

'75%...' I bargained.

'*Chal…pura packet rakh le, muh band rakhna bas…* (Take the entire packet…just don't tattle).'

Here's another one and most interesting one…Love Forges of High School. When it was the peak of this teenage love story, the butterflies flickered in the stomach when we got a glance of our crush. Talking and sharing lunch was so far, their just one glance was enough to make our day.

Many of us attended school in well-dressed and well-combed hair. One became tip-top, when this soft feeling was experienced by the teenagers, especially in high school. An innocent expectation took place in their heart, that one day, "they" will turn back.

During those good days, attendance was also improved, each day was important, just to enjoy that moment in which, the heart beat faster than usual. 'Love is in the air,' this line was proved, and even, felt in those high school days. His/her fragrance was just in the air, that's why, environment felt fresher.

Recess time…and we flicked to the basin. In no time, hands over hands loaded.

Chattering of students audible. Some classes had converted into fish market, while some were completely empty. A single tiffin, and overloaded hands…we used to do like this only. That was totally fun. The world war for that pickle was just awesome. But I was not used to taking lunch to school. I just kept bothering the ones who were busy having their lunch. Quite notorious I was. And within 5 minutes, final bell and teacher simultaneously took place. Then the faces of students, who were still busy having their lunch, and teachers, were worthy to see.

Sports period was a favourite to all. Whenever we saw P.T. sir stepping towards our class (as a substitute teacher) it felt like, 'Yes! Now at least for today, physics will not bother us.'

'Is it 10B?'

'No sir, 10A.' Usually class president replied.

The same song played in our hearts, '*chhhannn se jo tute koi sapna…* (When a dream shatters in a flash)'…it was more heartbreaking than a breakup. But, when it was our "authentic" sports period as per the schedule, whether the sky burst, or earth moved upside down, no power could resist us from moving to the ground. The sound of whoooosshhhh…of flying plates and that red ball of cricket, swimming in the lake…requesting for 5 more minutes to stay in the ground, and returning to class, making haunted laughs and nuisance in the corridors, the laughs and giggles we made…All these are still audible, whenever I take a glance of my high school, from my window or terrace. (It's just 10 steps away from my residence).

How can we forget our last periods? When only 15 minutes were left, our digital watch became the "rocket launch timer". 10min to go…9min to go…8min to go…and so on. The continuous murmuring, yawning, head down on the desk, packing bags before 10 minutes, some were busy in watching the landscapes outside the window. '*Class baahar chal rahi hai kya?* (Is your class going on outside?)' the common dialogue delivered by the teachers.

After listening to the tedious lecture of last period, finally, we got rid for today, a sigh of relief it was. Saying goodbye to each teacher who was standing to guard the rows of "monkeys", samosa party at the stall, cold drinks in sunny days are "refreshing" till today. And all those activities, neat and tidy uniform, scolds for eyeliners, hair gel and nail paints, whitening shoes with chalks, were going to repeat next day.

"Final bell" rang.

As the time passed, those "Next Days" became the "Last Day", and unwilling end of high school's journey took place. 'The journey, which starts, comes to an end also'.

It was the time to take leave, to say a teary goodbye. Now, those "buds" are full bloomed "flowers." This "Golden age" was about to finish. A "full stop" was stepping towards our high school's journey. "The Farewell" if not discussed, then in my opinion, it will leave the journey of High school incomplete.

A Grand Goodbye, a "mixture" of emotions, a tearful speech, outgoing students in their civil dresses: graceful sarees and formal blazers, funny skits and mimicry, precious throwbacks, and priceless best wishes from juniors and faculties, and also refreshments (to switch mood from sadness to flavours). All these made the Farewell most joyous, excited, melancholic and most memorable day of High school. It was actually, mixture of emotions, but it was more heartbreaking, as it was the time to take leave from the educational carrier of High school.

'Though, there was an atmosphere of joy and excitement, yet it was sprayed with fumes of melancholy.'

Teacher's scold, corridor's haunted laughs, chalk fights and pen fights, morning assembly, breaking queue…all these usual activities flash one after the another, whenever I see the playground of my school. At the end, a group photography, which will take us to our good, old days, whenever we will take a glance on it. Though, we got some lifelong friends and some special relationships, with special people.

'This day was the first time in the entire high school journey, that we were not in school uniforms, but, today onwards, this school uniform will be the "best dress" and will occupy a special place in the almirah.' Isn't it?

Wheel of time keeps moving, "flowers" leave to live another world, new "buds" fill the vacant branch of "Trees"…and this cycle continues, giving us a gift of "loads of memories."

The tea of memories will keep brewing on the flame till eternity, giving it a fresher taste, as per the time.

'Heart is heavy, wet are eyes,

Those nuisance and sweet, little lies.'

It's damn true…those were the days, the golden ones, the carefree ones, and "The Days to Relieve".

2.

## Sweet Nemesis

Tiyasa Tikadar

*Cute.*

That was the very first word that crossed my mind when I saw you for the first time back in third grade. You were sitting beside a guy who used to live in the same street as me.

*Short.*

That was the second word I thought of when I noticed our height difference when I passed by you one day.

*Rude.*

The third word that struck my mind when you talked to me for the first time, well kinda snapped at me for talking so loud in the class.

*I hope he chokes on his water.* I thought when you continued snapping at me for talking in general. Apparently, you were the class leader, and your job was to maintain pin-drop silence in the class and not let anyone talk (class teacher's order). And of course, you found me mumbling to myself as "talking" with my friends. And just because of your idiotic thought, I always ended up getting punished by our class teacher.

A month later, getting tired of your bullshit, I also decided to give you a taste of your own medicine. Whenever you told me to not talk, I snapped back at you. Whenever you glared at me, I glared back at you. If I was going to get punished for absolutely no reason, then I better get something good outta it. And that "something good" was nothing better than getting on your nerves, because you got on mine too.

In other words, whatever we had was raw hatred for each other. Hell, we even used to verbally bully each other and tried hard not to strangle each other (we succeeded). I even used to plot your death in my mind (horrifically weird I know). But our hatred for each other lasted for only one year. It wasn't until we were in fourth grade did I start feeling something other than hatred and despair for you.

I still remember that day. How we were seated far away from each other, how I felt someone staring at me, how I turned my head to check who was watching me, how our eyes met only for a few seconds, how suddenly we looked away from each other and how I realised that it was you who was watching me. That day I felt something inside my chest, and inside my stomach. I didn't know what it was in my chest, but I knew what it was inside my stomach. *Butterflies*, they said. I didn't look at you for the rest of the day, not even when you teased me to get a rise out of me. Only because I felt something other than hatred for you. And that scared me.

That day I went home and stared in the mirror. Then I whispered your name. And I swear I got them again. Those freaking butterflies. But this time, I ignored them. 'Cause I didn't want to catch feelings for you. But I did. I did before I realised it.

For the next few days, I dreamt of you. I dreamt of your warm chocolate eyes, your sweet smile, and your teasing words. And I knew I was a goner. I became someone different towards you a few days after I caught feelings for you. We still fought, but it was different. There was something sweet about our banters. We smiled and laughed at each other while fighting if that made sense. We helped each other whenever we could, laughed together at something funny our teacher would say, and even got punished together. We were friendly with each other. And somehow, I hoped you felt something for me too. Because I was in freaking love with you, nemesis. So much that I couldn't even describe it in words. I just knew that you were the one for me. And I wanted to marry you in the future. And have babies with you. Hell, I even decided how many kids I wanted and what would be their names. That's how crazy I was about you, my nemesis. So crazy about you.

My beloved nemesis, do you remember the bittersweet moment we shared back in the eighth grade? 'Cause I remember it clearly. The memory is as fresh as a field of daisies in my mind.

It was around early November. Winter had blessed the city we resided in at that time, resulting in us wearing blazers at school. Our class teacher assigned us to decorate our classroom for the school's 32nd anniversary. Much to my luck, you and I were given the same task; to make the paintings, as both of us were pretty good at it. For some reason, you weren't happy with the idea of us working together. And I didn't know why. But I brushed off the dejected feeling I got.

We were told to make five paintings if I remember correctly. I remember us starting on the paintings around $5^{th}$ period so that we didn't have to attend the rest of the classes that day.

We were painting in the art room, and you were standing far away from me, which made me a little bit sad. There wasn't anyone in the room but us, and that made my stomach do a little flip (in a good way). Because at that moment, only you and I existed. That moment was only for us.

Even though it was winter, you didn't bother to wear any blazer that day, so I ditched mine as well. Your hair was neatly combed, but still, a few strands fell over your temple. Your eyebrows were drawn together in concentration, your warm eyes fixated on your painting like it was a huge challenge. And damn if that didn't make you look dreamy.

I kept stealing a few glances at you in the beginning. But after a few minutes, I openly stared at you. You were just too precious to not look at. But much to my chagrin, you caught me staring at you.

You raised an eyebrow when you looked in my direction. 'Why are you looking at me like that?' You asked with a hint of coldness in your voice.

Shit. That was the only thing I thought before I mustered up a reply with a question. 'Like what?'

'Like I'm some interesting piece of art.'

*You are.* 'I'm actually looking at the interesting piece of art behind you.' I nodded at the painting behind you and internally sighed. I made a mental note to treat our art teacher with his favourite chocolate for putting that painting on the wall behind you.

You turned around and looked over at the painting before turning back to my direction and replying with an 'oh'. Several seconds passed away before you spoke again. 'Are you done with your work?'

I nodded back at you. 'It turned out better than I thought,' I said and looked back at my painting. All I had painted was a bunch of pink roses in a flower vase made of glass, with one of them laying on the table with a few scattered leaves instead of standing in the vase like the others. A part of me was scared to paint it, as I was never good with the flowers, but somehow it turned out beautiful. A smile found its way to my lips as I looked at the art I created.

'Really?' You were a little bit shocked by my words, knowing of my inability to paint flowers, no matter how hard I tried. 'Let me see.'

You left your work and made your way over to me. My heart started beating faster with every step you took towards me, and my hands felt clammy by the time you were standing beside me looking over at my painting. My heart was beating so loud I could hear it through my ears, and I was afraid you could hear it too. We were just three inches away from touching each other. And damn if that didn't make my heart beat faster than ever.

*That was the first and the last time you were ever so physically close to me.*

'That's....nice,' You commented.

A scoff left my lips. 'It's way better than *nice.*' I crossed my arms over my chest and kept my eyes on the painting. I couldn't look at you without doing something unforgivable to you.

You didn't say anything, but I knew you agreed with me. We just kept standing there silently and I started feeling self-conscious about myself. *Did I smell nice? Did my hair stink? Were my clothes clean?*

'I heard you have a crush on me.' You suddenly broke the silence with those dreaded words and my stomach sunk. *What?*

Panic washed over me, and I suddenly wished I could get far away from you. I didn't want to lie to you, but I didn't want you to know the truth, knowing it would hurt more. I let out a deep breath. 'Which idiot told that to you?' I hoped the fear wasn't evident in my voice.

'Vinnie was talking to Kiara about how crazy you go whenever I'm around you. I overheard them,' you explained and crossed your arms over your chest, but not before unintentionally brushing your warm hand against my cold one, which made electricity shoot through my veins and made me forget what you said for a moment.

I breathed out a laugh and God, it sounded so fake to my ears. I turned to face you and let my arms fall by my side. 'And why would I go crazy over you when I'm already crazy about someone else?'

When you turned to face me, a frown was etched over your pretty face. 'Fictional boyfriends don't count,' You stated.

I rolled my eyes at your stupid words. 'Well, in my case, they do.'

I gave you a shrug before continuing, 'And aren't you already head over heels for Niya? Why would I want you when you're already crushing over someone else?'

I meant it as a joke, but I didn't, couldn't ignore the way your pupils dilated, and a tinge of pink appeared on your cheeks the moment I said her name. My stomach dropped and fear consumed my heart.

'Wait,' I slowly and carefully said. 'You actually like her?'

You immediately replied, 'No! I don't!' Your voice shook and your lie was evident.

'But you're blushing hard there, dude,' I pointed out and gave you a fake amused smile.

Finally, you sighed. 'Is it that noticeable?' I could hear my heart crack the moment you said those words.

*Crack.*

*Crack.*

*Crack.*

I shrugged. 'Maybe.' It was evident you were absolutely head over heels for her. I never thought you'd fall for her, especially when she changed her boyfriends like a freaking calendar. Maybe you didn't deserve me, but you never deserved her. You deserved better, way better than her.

'That's cool,' I finally said and gave you a small smile. 'And you don't have to worry about telling me. I won't tell a single soul. After all, I'm your friend.'

You stared into my eyes. 'Friend?' You echoed.

I bit my lower lip. 'What would you say this thing we have is?' I waved my hand between us.

You remained silent for a few seconds, making me anxious, before giving me the smallest smile of yours. 'Friends.'

I smiled back at you real this time—and asked you to show me your painting. I was physically present there that day, but in my mind, I was screaming for you to love me and not Niya.

I was hurt, but I could understand. You'd never fall for me, no matter what I did to make you happy. 'Cause you were made for someone else. And I accepted that fact, even though it hurt like hell. At least we were friends. And that was enough for me.

Dear nemesis, I was asked which high school memory I'd want to relive. The thing is, I want to relive every memory I shared with you. But the time we spent that day, I want to relive that day the most. I want to relive that day and prevent myself from mentioning Niya in our conversation at all. I want to relive that day because I want to save myself from the heartbreak I got that day. I want to relive that day 'cause then I'd choose the truth and confess my feelings for you.

That day, the day I got my first heartbreak, I wished for something. I wished for us to remain friends forever and never become a stranger to each other like we are today.

3.

## That Place in the Memory Lane

Mouly Dangarwala

A lane of memories,

a way of life.

A ray of sunshine

with a path of strife.

High school,

the place where our memories reside,

full of moments that made up our lives.

That place, the one that found us partners of a lifetime.

When did it end, and where did it go?
The haven for some of those lost souls.
The place that marked the onset of achieving our goals.
The place that marked the beginning of adulthood,
and brought an end to our childhood.

Yeah, it is the same place that swallowed some as a whole,
having left them with a gaping hole.
The place, the one that didn't stop those who laughed at our cries,
The one that added more steps on our way to the skies.
The place that was full of secrets and fake smiles,
Was it an angel or devil in disguise?

4.

# Is it an End or a New Start?

Katyani Sharma

Leaving high school felt a lot like a senescent leaf,
can't hold on, yet unable to leave.
None of it will ever comeback, can you believe?
All the memories remain,
urging me to take a trip down the memory lane.
Is it an end or a new start?

Do you remember when all we wanted were good marks
and instead of studying, we used to count on our lucky charms.
The journey from first love to first heartbreak wasn't facile,
those random scribblings on the benches weren't futile.
Bunking lectures kept our bodies warm,
but now I feel cold.
Is it an end or a new start?

Every day, a new gossip travelled across the hallways,
backbenchers were always the highlight of the day.
Morning assemblies gave some a chance to witness their crush,
while some fainted under the morning sun.
Reminding the teacher about the test was a traitor's act,
study sessions turned into rounds of truth and dare was its counteract.
Is it an end or a new start?

All of it came at a price,
sleepless nights to be precise.
The shirt that was scribbled, oh, how can I forget?
I hoped "Friends Forever" was not just a myth.
Stepping out of this world is daunting,
but an independent life seems to be vaunting.

Is it an end or a new start?

5.

## Summer of Love

Rashmita Nayak

I saw you for the first time, with a stick in your hand,
You walked around the camp but you talked to none;
But the time when I understood you couldn't see,
My heart felt something between love and alchemy.

And then, you gave that million-dollar smile of yours,
A smile so beautiful, so contagious
Which made me smile even through my pain,
I'm sure the flowers around you bloomed again.

That's when I knew I had fallen so bad,
I didn't know if it was the summer air or love at first sight.
All I knew was that I was mesmerised, I was perplexed,
When I saw you looking so perfect, in that Yellow Floral dress.

I took a step forward, delighted to talk to you,
I followed you to the dance hall, a few minutes ago where I saw you walk through.
My eyes searched for you frantically, to see you dancing without fear,
That's when I realised, the attraction I had towards you wasn't just mere.

You danced around in the hall so gracefully,
You twisted and twirled and flew like a fairy.
I wondered for a second if the angels were following you around,
or you were an angel yourself that I had luckily found.

It was at that moment that I knew; I had fallen deep and hard,
So in-depth, so intense, like Alice in Wonderland.
And then when we finally talked for the first time,
My life suddenly felt like it was all sunshine and rainbows.

We spent our days together and our nights stargazing with you in my arms,

My eyes were your mirror, as I showed you the constellation of stars.

We talked for hours, we had finally grown close,

And I knew at that moment, that I wanted to protect you from the world.

And soon it was finally our time to leave,

We confessed our love and promised to meet.

We decided to meet on New Year's Eve,

On London Bridge, after your surgery.

You gave me your dream catcher that night,

And I gave you my favourite pendant;

We kissed, we cuddled,

We talked about our pain.

And I knew for sure, that you weren't just my first love,

But my love for eternity, and without you, nothing in this world would ever be enough.

I can't wait to see you see me, on New Year's Eve,

This summer of love was my best summer, the Summer of Seventeen.

6.

# We'll Be Okay

Jasmeen Bagga

Everyone gathered in the old school hall eyes my pink face as I get on my feet and saunter up the stage. I can recognise most of my old classmates and they seem to do pretty well for themselves.

Though… speaking in front of them seems as mind-numbing as it was back then. Cold, spider-like fingers race up and down my spine as I step onto the wooden platform.

I clear my throat and begin:

'Hey everyone. It is absolutely riveting to see you guys again after so many years, and clearly, shit has changed.'

A few scattered laughs echo in the room, making me smile.

'I will try to not take much of your time because I have been told in the past that I can be a lousy talker.

'The thing is, we all have gathered here tonight to cherish what we had over here in this school a couple years back, to reminisce and to relive the hardships, the good times and to share one of our life-changing tales from the time when we were just a bunch of naive teenagers. And I am genuinely happy to be here.

'I honestly loved all your anecdotes and I hope mine won't bore you guys either. When I was in high school, I wasn't exactly an outgoing person as most of you may remember. I was, in fact, on the brink of losing my actuality, but that didn't necessarily hint that I was not happy or something. I was. It's just that I thought it would be better to not be on the map.

'I remember, when I was seventeen, I fell in love with a girl who was my best friend. Well, my only best friend. Her name was Rue. You all remember the exchange student who came in the middle of Junior year? Yeah… her. She was amazing.

'A week before our graduation, Rue came up to me and made me forcibly go to what she told me was a stupid get-together. When I reached the destination, I couldn't help but feel an intense urge to murder her because it wasn't how I, or anyone for that matter, imagined a typical high school get-together to look like. At all. It wasn't even close.

'Let me walk you through it. There were a bunch of drunken teens making out in bathroom tubs, snorting drugs and smoking weed; meaning that Rue of course, had tricked me into coming to a high school party.

'I was so panic-stricken at first that I nearly sweat myself dry, trying to not move a muscle. So, my best friend took me to an empty bedroom upstairs and she—very respectfully— told me to cut the crap and have some fun.

'To quote her, "Can you please enjoy yourself for one night? I need this, for us. This is important to me."

"This is important to you?! Rue, you know I hate partying. Plus we can do this any other time. I just don't feel like enjoying myself right now," I'd rebelled with rage.'

I smile as I start reminiscing about that party that changed everything. Momentarily forgetting I'm giving a speech to all my old peers, I find myself taken back to that night… to the end of our school… to Rue.

****

## Years Ago, at the Party

'Why don't you get it? We can't do this any other time, beca…because I am leaving. I got my acceptance letter last week and I am leaving for California right after our graduation. I got into Berkeley, Casey.'

I was speechless at that point; the fact that she was leaving in less than a week made my heart drop. At that time, I had no idea what to do. I just knew that I didn't have enough time to overthink this, and fighting with her wouldn't be doing any good to either of us.

Among the two of us, Rue was the one who was more goal-oriented and determined. She'd sent her application forms to every top university in the continent months ago. She was too eager to leave this town behind. I didn't get it at first, but I did respect her decision. She often forced me to look for universities, too, so that I could get myself enrolled into a good med school. At first, I resisted, because even the thought of leaving my home and this life behind gave a nauseated feeling—yes, I was one emotional nutbag.

After her constant badgering, I eventually gave in and sent in my application to Albert Einstein College of Medicine, which was my dream school. I had zero hopes of getting in because it had an acceptance rate of only 4.3%, but then again, my GPA scores were close to perfect, so it wouldn't have hurt to give it a shot. I wanted to move out eventually, and I guess it was time, I thought to myself.

Anyway, I wanted to make that night special for the both of us and maybe tell her how I actually felt about her before she left.

I'd grabbed her hand and said, 'You are right. Let's make this count.'

I took her by the waist, and we danced around to our favourite song. That was the first time I actually learned to let go of everything else. I was dancing without the fear of people staring or judging me.

My hands were up high, touching the sky, and my body moved

like a rope slowly uncoiling itself.

Rue got us a couple of vodka shots, and we, for once, acted like regular teenagers. Vodka burnt my throat, but I was happy; in that one fleeting moment, I was actually happy because of her, and that day, my heart and throat both were on fire.

We danced through the night and eventually took a cab back to my place. My parents were off on some business trip, so we crashed at my place because she couldn't go home all liquored up, or else her parents would have kicked her out, once and for all.

We somehow managed to get into our PJs and zonked out as soon as our heads hit the pillow.

The next morning, I woke up with the biggest headache, but I was all in glee. The fact that I had tried something new felt good, weirdly good.

I rushed down to Rue, who was making our breakfast, and said, 'Thank you for last night. I enjoyed it a hell lot... and Rue, you know what? I know we have like 5 days until our graduation, but I want us to do a few more maniacal, normal teen things before you leave. I mean, if you want.'

Rue, who was still recovering from her hangover, gave me a pretty wide grin and said, 'Let's make a list then, Casey.'

We worked on our list, and we came up with 5 things:

1) Trying weed for the first time.

2) Staying out all night.

3) Doing karaoke.

4) Going to a carnival.

5) Stealing one of our parents' cars and driving off to Love Circle. (Rue's idea, not mine.)

I had one more thing marked in our checklist that Rue wasn't aware of.

It was confessing how I actually felt about her before she left.

The next few days were pretty wacky. We practically did things I wouldn't have dared to do if I were alone.

We went to a club and got pretty wasted and danced the night away. The disco ball light launched every shade of rainbow into the darkness of the night, and I felt euphoric waves rushing through my body.

Rue was a daredevil, and when it came to pissing her parents off, she was the first one to get in line. So, when it came down to stealing one of our parents' cars, I insisted on mine, because my parents were easy-going and wouldn't have made a big fuss out of it, but Rue was so hellbent on affronting her parents that she wouldn't have let me win without a fight.

So, we reached her place around 5 p.m. after getting her some leftover essentials from Target. She sneaked into their room when her folks were out for a nice evening walk with little Muffin, her Labrador, whom she had rescued from the streets when she was seven. She finally came back, and we hurriedly got seated. She inserted the car keys and off we went.

We drove for a few miles and turned to Hillsboro West End, finally pulling the brakes on Love Circle, which had the best scenic lookout of Nashville. We sat down on the moist grass and realised that it was almost dusk. The sun slowly drowned into the infinite sky, and it sparkled fire through every wintry hearth. The city never looked more beautiful.

I pulled out my iPod and untangled my earphones. I gave one to Rue and played Castle on the Hill by Ed Sheeran.

*And I miss the way you make me feel, and it's real*
*When we watched the sunset over the castle on the hill*
*Over the castle on the hill*
*Over the castle on the hill...*

I looked at Rue and smiled in awe of her beauty. She had the capacity to make death feel like a reward, and I…

I told myself to stop acting like an idiot around her and be cool.

'You are not an idiot, you know?' said Rue.

*Stay calm! Stay calm! Stay Calm!*

'I mean, you are perfect, Casey. I know going to these clubs, stealing and stuff might make you feel like one, but you need to let go sometimes. Every time you notice other people staring at you or when I force you to get your pictures clicked, I notice the same fear on your face—the fear of not being good enough. But Casey, have you ever wondered how perfectly and properly beautiful you actually are? You are perfect—I mean, you are kind, you are funny, a bit of a control freak, but you are more beautiful than I'll ever yearn to be. You just need to stop feeling sorry for yourself this once and let yourself be you.'

I held on to my breath for a second, and then I looked at her and said, 'I love you, Rue, and I promise to make these last days as memorable as possible for you. I mean, after all, it's you.'

'You better, fucker. You know I'll be the one burying you alive if you leave me out to dry.'

'You don't have to kill me, and I am not letting go of us.'

'I won't either, you know.' And with that, she hugged me tight, and the sun smiled at us through its orange-red sparks.

**The next day**

Rue and I went to the rooftop and karaoke bar where we had planned to do our first karaoke together. I was obviously terrified, because I had always been so anxious about myself when it came down to singing, or let alone existing in between a group of people, whereas Rue was thrilled because she had legit dreamt of doing this with someone one day.

We got our place reserved because it was a busy Sunday night and waited for our turn while the couple in front of us sang some classic hits of Taylor Swift. A few minutes later, everyone else sang along with them, and it started to sound a lot like an actual concert. When they were done, we walked up the stairs to a little brown, polished stage.

I took a deep breath and told myself to focus and tried to put my spirals of self-doubt back to rest.

I came a little closer to the mic and began without a second thought:

*The day that I met you*
*The world had just spit me out*
*On my way to the bottom*
*Sure I'd never be found*
*Then you saw me for me*
*Made me believe in myself*
*On the day that I met you*
*It all turned around*
*You said close your eyes*
*Don't look down*
*Fall into me and I'll catch you, darlin*
*We'll dance in the street like nobody's watching*
*It's just you and me and the song on repeat in my head*
*Playing over and over.*

Rue smiled at me, and it almost felt like she was telling me that she was proud of me for stepping out of my comfort zone, and then she followed up. And trust me, it was more fun than I had ever imagined it to be. For a while, it felt like there were just the two of us, and we sang without a worry.

We had our dinner in a nearby diner and came home at midnight.

I remember, as I was on the verge of falling asleep, I realised that Rue was leaving in 36 hours.

Soon, it was the last day. I had felt more alive in those 5 days than I had ever felt in my 12 years of schooling, and that pretty much summed it up.

Rue's parents weren't good to her from the very beginning. They'd wanted a boy, and when Rue was born, she was seen as a disappointment. I guess that was why she was so keen on moving away to Cali, and I didn't blame her for it. It did suffocate her to watch her parents fight every single day for the stupidest of things.

When she was little, she used to put her headphones on and play the music as loud as she possibly could to shut the voice of her father barking at her mother. She was also given the name Rue by her father because it meant to *regret*. It was a symbol of disappointment, and she had to carry it with herself forever.

'Casey, we have to go!' I heard my mum's voice echoing through the narrow hallway. I shook my head as I stuffed the pendant I got for Rue in my backpack and rushed downstairs.

My mom dropped me off at Rue's because she knew it was our last day together, and I assumed she wanted us to spend as much time as possible together before she left.

Rue was packing her last case of clothes and essentials, while I sat on the bed crossing things off her checklist.

'You think it will be okay? I mean, will I be okay all alone out there? What if we don't make it?'

She was partially hyperventilating without daring to look up into my eyes.

'Rue, you are the bravest girl I know. Hell, you made these last few days the best days of my life. You always make the best out of things, moments, and life. We'll be okay. I mean, it's us. I wouldn't find someone half as annoying as you even if I tried.'

We chuckled out loud and she addressed me with a *fuck you* which I deserved.

'Can I ask you something?' I bit my lip as soon as those words escaped my mouth.

'Yes. Anything,' she replied.

'That day, when we took your father's car up the hill, was he mad at you? I know how he is, Rue. There is no way he would have let it go.'

'You are right. He didn't.' She pulled her hair back and lifted her neck up diagonally.

I could see the red coloured marks around her neck. Her father had tried to strangle her because she stole his bloody car for one night to enjoy her last 5 days in her hometown.

Tears blurred her eyes, but she still tried to speak up. 'He tried to—to strangle me. He told me that he would have killed me already if I weren't leaving in 48 hours. He—he is happy that I am leaving. You know why I try to piss my dad off so much? It somehow makes me feel powerful. All my life, I have felt so weak in front of him—his constant bickering and beating has left me with nothing, Casey. I hate him so much. Whenever I did something I knew he wouldn't approve of—stealing his car, for example—it made me feel free and strong for just a little while—which is enough for me. It makes me feel like I have control over my life which I know I don't—he controls it; he always has. I hate myself for not having enough courage to actually stand up to him. But living in denial helps me feel like I do have a little integrity and respect left for myself.'

I hugged Rue as tight as I possibly could. I had never seen her this vulnerable and helpless before, and watching tears fall off her face broke my heart. I wanted to tell her that I would shield her and won't let him, or anyone lay a finger on her, but it wasn't my place to say all of those things. It just wasn't.

We went to the carnival around seven and Rue *had to* choose the most terrifying and death-defying rides for us.

The fantastic beasts ride almost gave me a heart stroke, and a lump in my throat pulsed as the ride gained speed. I was almost unsure if I'd make it back to planet Earth.

Rue, on the other hand, had the time of her life, because of course, giving your best friend a near-death experience is so amusing to some people.

When we surprisingly made it out alive, I told her that this experience would remain fossilised in my bones till the end.

We went to truckloads of rides, had a lot of crazy things including rainbow shaped cotton candy if I remember correctly. When it was almost midnight, we finally got our turn for the Ferris Wheel ride, which seemed like a huge victory in itself, considering the chunk load of people who were still waiting in that queue.

We handed in our tickets and took our seats. When it was all filled in, it started to move up with a little jerk at the beginning, but thankfully, there were only two people seated in each cabin of the wheel, which helped me feel a bit more comfortable for what I was about to do next.

'Sometimes, I feel like I am stuck on a Ferris Wheel. One minute, I am on top of the world, then the next, I am at rock bottom.' I let out a deep sigh.

At that moment, I realised that my underarms were already soaked in deep sweat, and my heart was palpitating vigorously.

'It's from "Love, Sam". Isn't it?' she asked while staring down the ride and munching on her favourite Flaming Cheetos.

'Yes. Rue, I need to tell you something. It's um... important.' She noticed the seriousness in my eyes and asked me what it was about.

'I—I like girls. I am queer, I—I am... I'm a lesbian.'

I didn't realise that I was hyperventilating until she held on to my trembling hands. Tears streamed down my face, and I guess it was because of the fact that it was my first time coming out to someone. I thought I knew that it wouldn't be easy, but I didn't actually realise how terrifying letting someone know this closeted part of me actually was.

She hugged me and I buried my head deep into her shoulder. I cried like a little baby in her arms for a while, but then I pulled it together for the sake of myself. I somehow managed to gain enough strength to say what I had been meaning to say for a long time without breaking or falling apart in the middle.

She cooed as she hugged me and said, 'I love you, you dumb fuck. I accept you in every way or state possible and I will do anything to make you not regret coming out to me and to make you comfortable. I'll be your rock, always. I promise. Don't be scared, Case. It's okay, I got you. You will be okay.'

'Rue, I... I like someone, a girl. I am completely in love with every part of her, and I don't want to sound cheesy, but it's true. I have never been in love before; hell, I have never even liked anyone for that matter. I know that you used to think that I had a secret boyfriend or something, or that I didn't trust you enough to talk about guys. The only reason why I didn't talk about them is because I didn't like them, and I was too big of a loser to tell you that I was in love with someone else all along. Rue, I—I am scared—you have been through so much already—with your dad and everything—I don't want to fuck us up—fuck you up by adding this onto your baggage.'

'Case, hey—listen to me. Nothing you do or say can fuck us up. I know this is hard for you, but aren't you tired of hiding all of this from me, from everyone, huh? And don't worry about my baggage and shit. Whatever you are and whoever you like will never be a baggage to me. I run to you for support, and I want you to confide in me, too. I will be here, I promise. Now, tell me who are you in love with? This is a safe place. You can talk to me about this, okay? And if you aren't comfortable enough right now, then don't. I won't get mad at you or anything. I just want to know one thing—is she—the person you like—hurting you in some way? I mean, is she good to you?' Her eyebrows were stiffened up high in concern and curiosity. She waited for me to speak while she gently rubbed her hand around my face as she wiped off my tears.

I took a moment or two to finally speak up. 'She is not hurting me, and yes, she is good to me in practically every state possible. I have been meaning to talk to you about this for a long time and now that you'll be off to Cali tomorrow, so I just have to let you know, for the sake of my sanity. I—I am in love with you, Rue. I have always been. I didn't even realise what love was until I felt it through you. You made me feel more alive and safer in these past few days than I have ever felt in this lifetime, and I feel free, and I am happy. Hell, I have been dying to feel this way for a long time and now I am finally happy.

'The way you smile while witnessing the most basic things makes them seem so extraordinary. When you first told me you were moving to California and we danced through the night, I felt like crying my lungs out at first, but then, I saw how happy you were, and I told myself that it's for the best.

'You brought light into my life, something I can't really explain, because even the term light seemed so foreign to me before you came into my life. I know that we are best friends and nothing's going to change that, but Rue, I can't help myself. Believe me, I did try a lot to not feel what I have been feeling, but everything led me back to you; it always has. Rue, I hate everyone else in the world but you. I still am not sure what love actually means, but isn't this what falling for someone actually means?'

I looked up as I tried to catch my breath... and saw Rue silently choking on her muffed-up cries. Colour had drained from her face, and her pupils were set deep on the ground. I felt a little more strung out at that instant, and I let out a little cry as I worriedly pleaded with her to say something.

A part of me wanted her to say that she felt the same way, too.

'Case, I don't know what to say. I love you; you know I do, but...' Rue tried to speak up, but her throat slowly closed off—almost as if it pierced needles around her voice box.

'But you don't feel the same way,' I completed her sentence because I didn't want to make this any harder for her.

'I don't want to hurt you, Case. I don't. It's literally the last thing I would want to do. You are the single-most important thing in my life, you know the crap my family puts me through, and at the end of the day, I just need you to be there by my side. It's almost as if you are my escape and I wish for anything but hurting you right now. I am sorry, I—'

Her voice quavered and she finally broke into a puddle of tears in a mere fragment of seconds.

At first, I thought that it was selfish on my part to confess what I had been feeling, when I knew that she would be leaving soon enough, but then again, I knew that I wouldn't be able to live with myself if I hadn't confessed. This way, I wouldn't have to lie to her or myself anymore. I could be finally myself with that one person who actually cared about my worthless existence.

'Don't be, please. *We'll be okay,* okay? Nothing has to change between us. We still are best friends. Don't worry, okay?'

I tried to find enough words, but all of my strength and courage had worn out. I felt completely helpless and vulnerable at that moment.

'Okay,' she said as she gently kissed my teary cheek, and with that, she put her head on my shoulder, and we both softly cried for a while as the stars and the moon hid behind the dark night sky. It was almost as if they knew that we needed to stay in this darkness for a little while, to heal, to learn, and to grow.

I opened my backpack and I gave her a pendant, the same one as mine. It had hope engraved on it.

'I know why your parents named you Rue, but I have a completely different meaning of your actuality. You gave me hope, something I have been craving to find for a long time. You helped me find it through yourself. You gave me something to hold on to.

*You are my hope, Rue.*'

******

'With that, she went to Cali the next day right after our graduation. And that was it.

'We stayed in touch for a little while, until we were all caught up with our uni workload.'

I blink away the tears as I wrap up my story and smile blearily at my old classmates.

'She's not here tonight, and I am glad she isn't, because this means she didn't look back, not even once. She moved on, from this town, from her family, from everything, but I am betting that she still has my pendant around her neck as she is hopefully living her perfect dreamt of life.

'I guess that's the thing about high school. These bittersweet stories are what makes us whole at the end. Falling in love, getting our heart broken, discovering new things about one's gender expression and sexuality, getting out of our comfort zone at least once, and finding who we really are. The week before my graduation will always be special to me, and so will Rue. She showed me how life is supposed to be lived, and even though she was struggling her way through it all, it never stopped her from starting over—from moving to California and not giving up on her dreams, and I guess that is what made her more real and less of a fairy-tale. And I am glad I had the balls to finally do the same.'

I finish my speech and look around. Surprisingly, everyone seems to be in awe and not bored at all, so that's a win for me. I walk down the stage and after the reunion, I sit on the rooftop, pull out my phone and hit play to that one damned song.

*And I'm on my way*
*I still remember these old country lanes*
*When we did not know the answers*
*And I miss the way you make me feel, and it's real*
*When we watched the sunset over the castle on the hill*
*Over the castle on the hill*
*Over the castle on the hill.*

7.

# I'm a Boy

Jasmeen Bagga

I forgot my binder.

Miss Jenn moved forward with her English lesson, but I couldn't shake the thought off my head. The idea of my breasts hanging off freely made me feel uneven—no, actually, that was an understatement. I hated my body and the way it made me feel. It might sound dark, but sometimes, all I wished to do was to chop off my breasts and be done with it.

'Ollie, are you even listening?!' Miss Jenn's angry voice brought me back from my reverie.

I zoned out a lot and that did get me in trouble, but then again, I couldn't help myself. 'Yes, Miss Jenn. Sorry, I was—'

She cut me off in the middle and continued, 'Meet me after class, but for now, go through page 57. I'd like to see you making notes for the same.'

I pled myself to focus and do the assigned task.

The bell rang.

Everyone hovered on top of each other as they left the classroom with a look of relief. I walked up to Miss Jenn and she told me to take a seat.

'So, how are you, Ollie?' She asked while marking our daily assignments.

'I am good, Miss Jenn. I am sorry about earlier. I was paying attention but in the middle, I kind of—'

She cut me off again and with a soothing tone asked, 'Do you still talk to him? Your father?'

His mention hit like a punch in the gut.

'Not since he moved out.' I tried to keep this talk as formal as possible but that didn't quite hint Miss Jenn that I wasn't up for talking about him.

'I am sure it must be hard for you—' Her voice weighed a truckload of sympathy, which I despised. 'Ollie—I have seen how close you were with your father, and this must be hurting you a lot. But just know that I am here if you want to talk about it or anything for that matter. Okay?' She said and gave me a soft hug at the end.

Don't get me wrong, Miss Jenn was helpful. She knew about my hormonal therapy and my transitioning before any of my classmates did, and she had always been so supportive about it. But I hated the fact that she still brought up my dad in our conversations.

My dad—the only person I could actually open up to, left me and my mother and moved out about 2 months ago. It was right after I came out to him. He couldn't accept who I was, which ultimately led to his departure to a hotel room on the west side.

I sometimes hated myself for not being what he wanted me to be.

*His little girl.*

It was kind of funny that we humans crave the most amount of love and acceptance from that one person who isn't ready to come on board—like it probably wouldn't even matter if the whole world cuts open their hearts in front of us. We would always wait for that one person to come around, even though deep inside, we'd know that it's a long shot.

Miss Jenn was worried that I might mess my grades up if I didn't strap on now, and she was right. Last week, I got a B+ on my English paper, and I have never been graded below an A. Don't even get me started on Science and History101.

I thanked Miss Jenn and walked my way through the narrow hallway, where my best friend Jaylin was waiting for me.

It seemed to be a bright sunny day, and I wanted to get some sun and have a little time to myself. So, I bid my farewell to Jaylin and went to a nearby park which I had recently discovered.

I laid on the warm grass and shut my eyes. This feels nice, I thought to myself.

I loved myself, except for my skin and for the fact that my soul was literally trapped in the wrong body. But I did love myself and told this to myself almost every day just to level up my scraped-off self-esteem.

*I love who I am and regardless of what anyone says or believes, I am a boy.* I repeated it to myself like a mantra.

I came out to my class on my first day of senior year, which was almost two months ago, right after I came out to my parents. My dad moved out that weekend, and I wasn't actually ready to tell everyone, but after he left, I felt numb—I thought nothing anyone could do or say could make me feel any worse about myself. But boy does the universe surprise you.

I wasn't allowed to use the boy's restroom because, of course, I wasn't.

I heard some kids say, 'You are not a real boy. Stop kidding yourself,' and stuff like that all the time.

I was used to hearing these remarks because I knew that this was my life now.

I opened my eyes and got up. I rested my back on an old Scots Pine tree. Tiny birds were fed by an old couple nearby, next to which I saw a girl reading *"Call me by Your Name"*, which was one of my favourites. She looked at me and gave me a vague smile, and I couldn't help but smile back.

She came up to me a while later and introduced herself. Her name was Jenny. We started talking, and it led us to a good jogged off conversation.

'So, do you come here often?' I asked.

'No, uh… I wasn't feeling well, and there were some things bothering me, so I thought I should take a walk outside and maybe read something.'

'I am sorry to hear that. Do you mind telling me what it's about?' I asked out of social construct, but at the same time, I was hoping she wouldn't leave me hanging.

'It's my mother. She was drunk the other night and abusive. I couldn't get what happened out of my head.' Her voice quavered in between. I held her hand and worriedly said, 'I am sorry to hear that.'

'It's alright. So, what were you doing here? I am sure laying half-dead in the middle of the day is not your ideal definition of fun.' She asked with a touch of sarcasm.

I told her that I was kind of feeling blue because of my low grades. I also told her that I am a male transgender and I am on testosterone therapy and will hopefully transition eventually.

I told her about my father, which was highly unlike me. I had barely talked about any of this with Jaylin.

The fact that we are more comfortable telling a stranger our most closeted tales than our loved ones always seemed to baffle me.

******

*'You're not a boy!' My dad screamed at me at the top of his lungs.*

*'I am. I am a boy.' Tears streamed down my face, and I couldn't*

*understand what was more painful at that moment—the thought of living that way my whole life or the thought of losing my father because of who I was.*

*He took me by my arm and pushed me in front of the mirror. 'Open your eyes and look.' My eyes were shut to let the tears flow easily and he shook me hard. 'I said, open your goddamn eyes and look!' At his hard tone, I abruptly opened my eyes. I blinked through my tears to see the mirror clearly.*

*'What do you see in the mirror? A girl or a boy?' he asked me mockingly, and I pleaded with him to stop. 'What's this?' he pointed to my chest and demanded.*

*'Breasts,' I whispered, whimpering.*

*'Exactly! You're a woman. A girl. My baby girl. I've loved you with all my heart, so why are you punishing me, and for what?'*

*His words were like sharp silver bullets and I was a half-torn paper. What chance did I even have to stand my ground in front of him?*

*I fell to my knees, crying in agony as the night moved along, and my parents fought over me like they had never before.*

******

I shook that memory off my head and somehow managed to hold in my tears.

Jenny held my shaky knees and said, 'I am proud of you, Ollie, and no matter what anyone says, you are a boy—a pretty boy. What are your pronouns, if I may ask?'

I proudly said, 'He/him, and they/them, and don't call me a pretty boy. It's weird.'

'Pretty man?' She pouted.

'No! Stop saying that,' I rebelled in disagreement.

'Then what?'

'Nothing. I am just Ollie, and I am a boy, that's it.'

'Okay, pretty boy it is.' We both chuckled at that. The fact that she didn't say things like 'I am so sorry' or 'Just hang in there' or any of that sympathetic crap made me feel more accepted.

We sat there for a while, and I noticed her face showered in bright sunlight. I traced the way her lips moved when she talked, the colour of her eyes, and how her cheeks radiated baby pink light. It all was so perfect.

She was so perfect.

We talked for like 4 hours. I reached home by 6 p.m. and got a good scolding from Mom. I told Jenny that I'd meet her the next day at that very place and I took her number, just in case.

I spent most of my days, hours, minutes with Jenny. She visited my place a couple of times, and my mom loved her.

I felt this surreal peace of mind when I was with her. The kind of security you get when you actually believe that it will all be alright one day. She helped me keep that faith.

I couldn't help but accept the fact that I had started to develop feelings for her. Some serious fucking feelings.

It was on a Wednesday afternoon when I had encountered an incident with some guys from my grade. They called me names and said that I would still be up for fun if I'd been given a chance, so I shouldn't kid myself with this trans stuff.

'They said that I wasn't a boy,' I said with a low voice. I didn't care what people had to say about me, but sometimes, it did get too much.

Jenny rested her head on my chest and my fingers slowly brushed through her hair as we lay under the bright infinite sky.

She lifted her head and looked at me and said, 'I believe that you are a boy. A pretty handsome one, too, to be specific. Ollie, you are whatever you desire to be. It took you 17 years to finally transition into being what your soul has desired to be ever since your birth. You are a real boy, Ollie. I believe it, you believe it, your mom believes it, and that's all that matters. It might sting like a bitch to hear such remarks every now and then, but know that when you let yourself feel bad about who you are, they win. You lose because you are hating your soul for being what it desires to be. Be proud of who you are. Be yourself, Ollie, and if you need a little support then you'll always have my hand to hold. I love you in every way possible. Hold on to that, okay?'

*And I knew I loved her. I really loved her.*

'I love you, Jenny. I really do.' Finally saying it out loud filled me with confidence and anxiety all at once.

'I love you too, Ollie, you pretty boy.' She gave me a little chuckle and I smiled at her in return.

I wasn't sure if she said what she said to me as a friend or something else. Before I could overthink it, she placed her lips on mine. I kissed her with an equivalent amount of passion and in that moment, I couldn't wish for anything but this. I dwelled in our forever like a dying fish finally making its way back to the water.

That night, I realised that I finally had a girlfriend. An actual girlfriend, whom I loved dearly. The thought of Jenny gave me goosebumps, and I knew that these chills weren't going to fade off anytime soon, so I drank onto the thrill like some thirsty beast.

She kissed me diamonds that Wednesday, and I wore it around my neck like a trophy ever since.

**8 months later**

I checked the calendar and realised that it was my father's birthday. I wanted to talk to him, but even the thought of us in the same room made me feel weak and nauseated.

Jenny was about to come to my place to watch a movie, so I

shook his thoughts off and got ready to see her.

The testosterones I had been taking worked big time. My shoulders were all broadened up and tight and my voice had become deep. I felt more in place, which helped me look at the bright side for the most part.

Jenny and I sat on the couch as we scorched through Netflix to find a movie we both could enjoy.

'Hey.'

I heard a familiar tone from behind.

I looked around and my eyes met Dad's.

I couldn't move. My arms and my legs were frozen.

He walked up to me and sat in front of me.

'Who's she?' He asked, while pointing at Jenny.

'My girlfriend,' I replied rebelliously.

He snorted at my reply and rolled his eyes.

'Oh… so you still aren't over the whole trans thing.' He opened his mouth to let out a little smirk, meaning he was knowingly gaslighting me.

'Get the hell out.' I screamed. Anger burst through my veins and at that moment I hated him.

'I am your father. You can't talk to me like that!' He banged his hand on the couch.

'Yes, you are, but if you were a good father, then you would have accepted me!' I was trying to find some kind of love or compassion in his eyes, but then he said,

'I am not going to take part in this nonsense.'

'This nonsense? The fact that I had to live in a body that's not even mine to begin with for 17 fucking years is not nonsense. The fact that I had to act like a girl for you to accept me is not nonsense. I did that for you to accept me. I knew I wasn't a girl all these years, but I kept it to myself because I was scared of this—of what exactly happened. You told me that you loved me no matter what. Well, Dad, don't say such things if you aren't going to mean them. I am bullied almost every single day and get called names worse than you'll imagine. I don't do this for fun. I don't do this because I enjoy it. I do this cause that's who I am, and I am fighting for myself. I needed you to help me fight this battle, because I knew that I was too weak to fight it on my own. But you abandoned me—you abandoned Mom and you left us. I hate you for it. I hate you so mu—' My throat jabbed pins around my voice box, and I couldn't say no more. I was done.

'I am sorry. I came here today because I wanted to tell you that um—that I accept you. But seeing those hormones work I just... You have to understand that this is difficult for me to come to terms with. But I swear I'm going to try. I love you. I have thought about you all these months, and I did miss you. I mean, after all, you are my kid. But I am transphobic, and I am willing to work on that. I accept you, but I hate the umbrella you are under at the same time, and I know it's messed up, but I want to be a part of your life. I want to be your dad... if you would want me to. I want you to give me another chance... son.' He said with tears falling off his face and I couldn't resist but hug him.

******

Dad and I bonded well over the next few months, and he finally became more accepting of the LGBTQ+ community. He somewhat even went overboard with it. He put rainbow-coloured flags around our mailbox and bought himself a PROUD DAD tee. Jenny thought it was quite cute, and I guess it was.

On the day of my graduation, I brought Jenny along with me to school to introduce her to everyone as my girlfriend and to show her around my campus.

My parents were there, too, and in between the crowd, some guy said,

'A girl with another girl while pretending to be a boy. Society really has changed.' I didn't bother with it but dad for once spoke up, 'He is a boy, you little shit.'

Miss Jenn heard him and asked the guy to leave. She then walked up to me and gave me a warm hug before going up to the stage.

The graduation ceremony began, and my turn finally arrived.

Miss Jenn spoke, 'Next is Mr Ollie Gilbert. They have always been a hardworking student, and I am really glad to get to know you, Ollie. Congratulations.'

My parents and Jenny cheered with joy.

When I went down the stage, Jenny rushed up to me and asked, 'Do you want to celebrate graduation over some drinks, pretty boy?'

'You bet, my lady.' And with that, we kissed through the sparkles and wine that floated around in the thick air.

8.

# My Snow-flaked Love Tale

Jasmeen Bagga

Gasping through our faded folklore

December whispered in my ear, yet again.

Reminiscing the streets

and sunsets, to the first time when

I saw *you*, my beloved Guinevere Beck.

Winds roared through the clouds

Deafening my thin earlobes

right into our spine.

Her grace tangled in deep,

Way as our hands enclosed within.

Our souls preyed and feasted a wild devour,

As I held onto her through Christmas Eve

Singing in the carols for the first time,

Joyous festive wrapped all over me.

Angels chirped in joy
Beasts roped in awe,
Both above the sky and below the sea
Existed as it was meant to be.
*But*
Hope perished the moment she dissolved in black and white,
I looked for her into the infinite sky and above,
In hopes of being able to be saved again
I flipped over every leaf and stone.
Yet, she left with no faded clue or stroll.
I blamed the angels, the demons, the chills, and the snow
Because without her, who was I meant to be?
I welcomed in the dark shadows again,
Moonlight bounced off my quivered lips
As I sat beside the white trees
I woke up to a cold Christmas light
Holding on to her necklace,
I buried in my tear some plight.
She left me with skulls of memoirs
I still carry within myself
So vast, it could cover an entire sea.
I crawled back to the same old town
Where time is slowed to stills,

On the same 47B Street

Under the old night light.

Witnessing constellations scattered over the dark sheet

I found you, in my beloved Cassiopeia.

My Love,

I snuggled myself in your owlsome light

Suffusing my sore eyes to rest.

I yearned to feel that way all over again.

The chills, the pain, and the stars were

long bagged in my cottage-shaped heart.

I craved to feel some emotion—any emotion except this hollow lump

pressing against my throat,

Something to save the brisk of my fractional existibility

Draining in my will to feel whole again.

I still remember the way

Her enchanting smile broke through her soft, cherried lips.

Keeping it safe within, I walked a step or two

In reverse to the time

I discovered the power of love and faith

Belief and magic, but mostly, *her.*

Winter swam into the frozen lake through cracks of radiant moonlight

And when we kissed on the scarred glass

Feeling her touch,

Through her lips to breathing in her air

I still remember the way she felt in the first fall of that snow-flaked town

And I soaked into that season like a thirsty dish rag

Carrying her taste,

With me to North America

Revisiting—her tongue discovering my soul and my lips worshipping her holy grace.

9.

## Swinging With Nostalgia

Ananya Duggal

My abdomen replete with fireflies,

Swinging with mirth while walking for miles,

From my residence to the buzzy life,

Of high school and friends' sly vibe.

So exciting, yet so frightening

At the thought of duping and

At the sight of professors muting.

A new feeling in my heart singing,

Every day as the high school bell ringing,

With a slight of lessons skipping,

And at the end of the day, being caught at the cafe dipping.

A feeling of mirth,

For being old enough to think better, and

young enough for being pardoned for chatter.

My abdomen replete with fireflies,

Swinging with nostalgia while walking for miles,

In the buzzy high school life,

Saying goodbye to the sly vibe,

And knocking the door of college time.

10.

# To My Soul Like Eclairs

Ananya Duggal

Today, I am sitting on a wooden chair,
With the blackboard in front of me sheer fair.
The sight of chalks and dusters,
fountain pens and paper,
preachers and breachers, learn and laugh,
tasting to my soul like eclairs.
I blink my eye, and the school bell cries,
'Bang Bang'—time for food tang,
Feeling yum in my tum,
As I eat the lunch sent by my bestie's mum,
Which brings my hunger out of its glum.
'Hurry, break is over,' thundering the thunder,
It's time to do a blunder,

Skipping the class and entering into a cafe slumber.

Nabbing, I say, as the teacher is catching,

A tint of blue blush, and a hint of mischievous rush,

I reach the classroom in a hive,

Seeming to be pretty naive,

Heaving a sigh of relief,

As the day ends with a retreat.

Oh! How well I remember the first day of high school,

Tasting to my soul like eclairs.

11.

# O Captain!

Sakshi Khillare

It is a fact universally acknowledged that your alarm will refuse to ring on the day you need it to ring on time.

Out of all days, I missed the school bus today. Yet, I somehow managed to reach fifteen minutes before the event began. Well, technically, I had reached half an hour later than the assembly event time.

Gathering my thoughts and my things, I stepped out of the rickshaw. Unfortunately, the rickshaw driver didn't have change, so I asked him to keep it and rushed to the gates.

Upon reaching, I noticed that there were a few students who were late and were lingering in the hallway.

'Keep your distance! Keep your distance!' The head girl's voice echoed in the veranda as I jogged past the students who stood in the line waiting for their turn to enter the assembly hall where the annual event would be taking place.

Taking two stairs at a time, I clutched my notepad under my arm and made my way to the hall.

*Dear universe, please save me today*, I silently prayed.

I pushed my square rimmed glasses up my nose and approached

my teammates backstage. I sneaked a glance at the clock, there were still fifteen minutes for the bell, which meant we still had time to do a quick rehearsal. Not only that, but I noticed that the helper staff had already begun setting up chairs for the audience and the other guests.

When I saw the crowd gathered around our class teacher, Miss Asha, I could sense that something was wrong. Someone nudged my shoulder, and I whirled around. It was Krita, my best friend.

'Miss Asha is in a mood today, isn't she?' I whispered to her as I scanned the crowd in the hall.

The words she spoke next did nothing to make my worries less. 'The narrator is absent,' she said, pursing her lips.

'What?' I almost yelled and then looking around, whispered, 'Why?'

'Miss Asha informed us that Tara has caught a nasty flu and that she won't be able to make it today,' Krita explained, worry visible on her face.

Closing my eyes, I released a slow, quiet breath. 'Now what?'

She shook her head and tugged at my arm, 'Now, we go talk to her and the team.'

In the backstage, all the participants had circled around our class teacher who was instructing them in her calm voice. As soon as we joined them, one of the girls came forward with her hands on hips. 'Look who finally decided to show up!' Payal bit out, looking pointedly at me. I grimaced at her tone and apologised, to which she scoffed.

I know she didn't mean it; she was just as panicked as the rest of us. This performance was as important to her as it was to me. I couldn't really blame her.

'Guys, let's just talk about the matter at hand.' Miss Asha broke the awkward silence and continued, 'Tara is absent, but we need a narrator.' She turned to me and tilted her head sideways as if confirming from me.

'Uh yes, Miss, you—right, you. We need a narrator.' I stumbled on my words.

'Sia, since you directed the play, I'm sure you're well versed with the script,' her voice held high hopes. Hopes that I didn't want to crush. But I knew where this was going, and I wasn't liking it one bit.

Miss Asha narrowed her eyes at me and scratched her chin, 'So, I think you should do the narration.'

'Me? Yes, I mean, yes, I will do the narration...' God knew what I was doing, but I couldn't disappoint our team. We'd practised for hours. Each one of us, including the ones who made the presentation, had toiled hard for this event. I couldn't let it all go to waste.

She shot me a wide grin and clapped her hands, her silver bangles clinking, 'Great then. Problem solved. Sia, go through the script with your team. We don't have much time left for the rehearsal. I will see you on the stage.' And with that she left to join the teachers.

As told, I tried to discuss with the teammates but they'd all scattered.

I took a seat on one of the benches and massaged my temples. How could one possibly deal with this situation?

I felt a tug at my braid, and then Krita flopped down beside me. She took one long look at the script in my hand before skimming mindlessly through the papers. 'Seriously, Sia, don't fret over it. It's going to be alright. We've got this.' She assured while inspecting the cuffs of the formal shirt all of us were wearing.

'Easy for you to say. You practically grew up on stage.' I voiced my thoughts.

'Ah, that would be an understatement. I was born for this.' The idiot continued anyway, having the audacity to crack jokes even in such a situation. But she was right. Krita was a phenomenal actress.

Right then, a bulb sparked in my mind.

'Then why don't you do the narration? You're confident, you have the charisma—'

'The charisma?' her brown eyes widened with surprise.

*Such a drama queen, I tell you.*

'And you don't have stage fright,' I mumbled, looking away.

But judging from the realisation dawning on her face, she probably heard that. 'Oh, so it's about stage fright. Didn't know you were afraid of the audience, Director Ma'am.'

Another word from her and I would outright start sobbing. My dilemma must've been obvious since Krita sighed, clearly giving up on goading me.

'Look, Sia, I may be good on stage, but I only know my part. And 15 minutes aren't enough for me to go through the rest of the script.' She clucked her tongue. 'You're on own.'

Fifteen minutes and five seconds later, I was truly on my own.

My hands trembled as I stood behind the podium. I clenched my clammy palms into fists. Looking at the huge crowd gathered, my mind started buzzing with a thousand different thoughts soon followed by the ringing in my ears. Somehow, I managed to keep my cool and plastered a smile on my face, but on the inside, my heart was thundering in my chest.

Suddenly, it didn't feel cold anymore. Drops of sweat beaded my forehead. Unclenching my fists, I jerked my chin and straightened the mic. Taking deep breaths didn't help. Hundreds of eyes were on me, and here I was, trembling like a rat caught in a trap.

From my periphery, I saw Miss Asha signalling me to begin.

So, I put the paper down and looked at the audience instead with a smile plastered on my face.

'Good morning,' I greeted, my voice too shaky. 'Good morning!' I tried again, this time a little louder.

The response was immediate. I managed a smile and continued, 'Respected Principal, honourable guests, teachers, and my dear friends, we've gathered here today on the occasion of tourism day.'

I gulped, feeling shitless scared.

*What was next, Sia? Introduction? Perhaps a funny opening line?*

I bit down on my tongue and grabbed my script again. I couldn't do this. I couldn't even speak without fumbling. 'Our... our grade is per—'

I was cut off by the sudden darkness that enveloped the hall. Immediately, the audience started mumbling amongst themselves, the helper staff rushed in a frenzy, perhaps to figure out how the electricity went out despite the generator.

My shoulders drooped as I stayed glued to my position. If the electricity was out and the generator wasn't supporting, then that meant I'd still have time to get myself together.

I rushed backstage where all of our team was already in chaos. Miss Asha was in a hurry. 'Here's what we're going to do. I'm going to explain this mind-blowing last-minute plan to our teammates and you, Miss Sia, are going to arrange costumes for us. Now shoo.' She practically shoved me out of the hall and went back to deal with our team.

Krita placed her hands on my shoulders. 'Sia, look at me.' I had embarrassed myself in front of almost the entire school. How could I look at anyone?

'Please.' she added calmly. 'I am looking at you right now. I see someone who is afraid.'

That made me look at her.

'I see someone who is afraid but won't run away,' she said in her ever-soothing voice. I regarded her before slipping back into the bathroom to get changed. A few minutes later, I emerged, dressed up in my shirt, the borrowed trousers tucked into the boots which I had very sweetly convinced our watchman uncle to lend me and the red sash of our school uniform tied round my forehead that would make up for the bandana.

I cleared my throat to get Krita's attention. She looked up from the laptop where she was working on our presentation. She leapt out of her seat, whistling.

'*Haaye meri* Jack Sparrow. (Aww my Jack Sparrow.)'

Before I could say anything, the bell rang and we both rushed to the assembly hall. Everyone in the audience had already settled. The dancers of our team had taken their positions.

I blew out a breath.

I could do this.

I stepped on the stage, my pirate-ish boots smacking against the floor. Instead of going behind the podium, I took the mic and stood in the centre. 'AHOY! Welcome everyone, who has boarded my ship today! I am Captain Sia and this—' I waved behind and Krita walked in, bowing in a dramatic way, before pretending to stumble.

'—is her navigator. Krita.' She introduced herself.

The audience cheered with a whoop which in return boosted my confidence.

And thus began our pirate-styled world tour. We first showed the audience the land of jewels, India. Then came the land of rising, Japan, followed by Australia. We passed by the land of pyramids, Egypt. We saw ancient Athens and then finally took a pit stop at the harbour in the United States. All of it just through a presentation.

I looked back at Krita, who was moving around with the binoculars (again borrowed from our laboratory) in her hands. She noticed me and shot a grin.

'We did well.' I mouthed to her and all the teammates who had choreographed a last-minute dance to a Celtic song.

Finally, when the event got over, I found Krita flopped lazily on one of the chairs. I sat beside her and removed my bandana.

'I am hungry,' she mumbled with her eyes closed and head rested back.

'Are you now?' I poked at her ribs.

'Yes. I think I'm going to die of hunger.'

'No, you're not.' I stood up and pulled at her sleeve. 'Come on, Navigator, let's get us something to eat.'

She got up and threw her arm round my shoulders, 'Aye, aye, Captain.'

12.

# Let's Breakup!

Namrata Prajapati

'Let's break up!' I suggested.

'What? Are you crazy?' Nex growled.

'No, I'm not. And the breakup is the solution for our problem,' I said, keeping my voice neutral.

We were sitting in the library, the fucking library. The place where we once met, fell in love, and started dating and now, we were almost breaking up. Good thing that I was a sucker for cliches, now that I had something to tell others.

'Look, I know I just dropped a bomb on you, but sweetheart, we can do better,' Nex said.

'Bomb? Nex, you're saying you can't do long distances. Seriously? Two days before our graduation? That's worse than a bomb,' I said through my gritted teeth. If it wasn't for the library's sake, I would've screamed in his face.

Nex was going to business school in California. I knew this when I started dating him ten months ago. I always knew he had planned his life, and I was always supportive of it. We had talked for hours in my backyard about doing long distances and we agreed that we could do this. I didn't know what changed his decision, but it was pissing me off.

'Claire, I'm sorry, but I talked to my cousins about our long-distance thing. I wanted to be hundred percent sure if this works or not, and trust me, it hurts to know that all of them said it doesn't really work.' I gasped, not because of how low chances we had to save our relationship but by how he had lost faith in us.

'We can change that. If you and I go according to our plan, we can make this work.' *For god's sake, Nex. Please make up your mind.*

'I don't know what to say. Take your time and think. We have two more days. I'll see you tomorrow.' He kissed my cheek and left.

Nex was the class representative, and I was just a simple girl. Our paths had never crossed until the last Christmas holidays.

We met at a store where we chose the same watch. I wanted it for my dad, and he wanted it for himself. It took us two hours; we fought, we mocked, we bribed, but at last, he gave up. I ended up buying the watch while he sulked next to me. Afterwards, I found his number through the school group and thanked him. It was just an excuse to talk to him.

He ignored me for two days. He was a jerk at first but eventually replied.

Days went by quickly, and I forgot how effortlessly I caught feelings for him under the blanket of warm friendship. More than friends and less than lovers. It was always an unspoken attraction until we sat in the library one evening and played a little game.

We scribbled sentences that came to our minds as soon as we closed our eyes.

'I hate cold,' he wrote.

'I smell silence,' I wrote.

'Your curls look like noodles,' he wrote and I burst into laughter. I almost forgot we were in the library.

'Your shirt looks nice,' I wrote, and he smirked, mouthing me a "thank you".

'Okay, now let's write the next sentence together,' he said, and I nodded. We looked at each other and I licked my lips in nervousness.

'I like you,' he wrote.

'Nex, let's date,' I wrote.

We showed each other and there were several chuckles.

The happy ones, the shocked ones, and the excited ones.

I had so many good memories with him that I basically daydreamed about a married life with him. I know it was silly, but this was Nex and me. And now, even though I suggested that we should break up, I didn't think I could do it.

It was the day before graduation, and I was at the library again. I ignored Nex for an entire day, so today, he called my mom's phone, and I had to answer because none of our family knew we were about to break up. If they knew, they would talk us out of it, and we didn't want that. We wanted to make decisions on our own. Decisions that might break us. Or just me.

'Hey!' He handed me my coffee while I glared at his face. His green eyes told me he didn't sleep much while his hair said that he had messed them up while wearing his hoodie.

'Did you sleep at all?' I asked, skipping everything else.

'Three hours max.' His tall frame settled down next to me.

'Claire, I thought about your suggestion, and I think…' he paused, fidgeting with my curls. 'I think you're right.'

My heart cracked and my eyes teared up but I controlled myself.

'Good! It's best if we break up mutually,' I said—more like whispered.

'Yeah, and I want you to live your life to the fullest, even if it means you will forget me.' His words poisoned me.

'Same goes for you.' I sighed heavily. 'Okay then, let's break up.

We need a story. I don't want anyone to think we broke up because you're leaving.'

'Don't worry, no one will pity you.' He cupped my cheeks, and I smiled.

'So, what do you think we can break up on?'

'I cheated on you!' he replied with a disgusting frown. I stared at him, my eyes moving up and down his face. I scoffed and he chuckled.

'That's the most awful idea, Nex. No one will believe us.' I chuckled.

'Okay, what about I killed your best friend?'

'Terrible!'

'I mistreated you.' I shook my head. Straight away a lie.

'You don't communicate.'

'No lies, something painful.' I pouted.

'Ugh! You're such a snobby…' I eyed him and got up. He wasn't taking this seriously.

'Claire!' He followed me. He was laughing while he hugged me from behind.

'I'm sorry. I was just kidding, you're my sweetheart.' He kissed my hair and tickled my waist which erupted a loud giggle.

'Stop! Don't tickle! It hurts!' I protested but he continued. At that moment we forgot that we had to break up.

******

Finally, it was graduation day. The anxiety had settled in me from dawn. I had been wide awake, staring at my ceiling. I tried listening to songs but stopped when the lyrics were starting to sound too relatable.

I tried doing yoga at 5 a.m. but couldn't do it for more than five minutes. It took me all morning to get ready at the speed of a turtle. And when I was finally ready, I stared at my reflection.

I looked pretty, but something was missing.

'Wear your smile, sweetheart!' I jumped back.

'Nex! What are you doing here?'

'I came to pick you up.' His fingers brushed my collarbone. 'You look gorgeous.' He kissed my temple.

'The blazer suits you.' I brushed his hair and he winked.

'Let's go!' he said, taking my purse. He walked out, and I picked up the present I had bought a month ago.

When we reached school, everyone was seated.

Once the graduation started, I didn't see Nex until he was called on stage. Everyone cheered as he had to give a speech. The crowd cheered for his confident and humorous speech.

'Claire!' Ian, Nex's best friend, tapped on my shoulder.

'Yeah?'

'Nex is waiting for you at the library,' he squealed. What a weirdo.

'Okay, thanks!' I headed to the library. I walked to our usual seat. There he was, tapping his right leg nervously.

'Congratulations, Nex!' I grinned as our eyes met. His lips curled up in a smile.

'Well, the degree suits you, Claire.' I blushed.

'Thank you… so, why are we here?' I raised my brow, and he stood up.

'Claire, I have to…'

'Wait!' I interrupted. I pulled out the white box. He raised his brow, and I pushed it in his hand.

'This is for you. I know you loved it, so I got you the same one.' He opened the box. It was the same watch we fought for.

'Thank you, sweetheart. This is amazing, I love you,' he said as quickly as he pulled me into the tightest hug. There were emotions, so many of them. I understood them all.

'I love you, Nex. We can do this. You and I can do this.' I said softly, kissing his neck, then jaw, and finally his lips. We stayed like that for a minute, slowly burning into the kiss.

When we finally pulled back, our eyes were moistened.

'So, what did you want to say?' I asked and he chuckled.

'Nothing serious. I got you this badge.' I opened the box, and the badge said

"Sweetheart".

'Aww, I love this. Thanks!' He took the badge and put it on my teal green dress. 'What time is your flight? I'm coming to see you off.'

'By 7 p.m. Be on time, okay?' I nodded, 'Anyway, I should go home and get ready. I need to do goodbye shit with my parents and cousins, too,' he huffed.

'Okay, see you later. Bye!' I waved at him as we walked out of the library, and he turned in the opposite direction from me. 'Nex, I love you, and you're the best,' I yelled, and he waved at me while still facing his back.

I went home and changed quickly. I looked at the time. I still had half an hour. I had to reach by 6 p.m., so I drove to the coffee shop, bought his usual drink, and headed towards the airport. Florida's traffic sucked!

By the time I reached the airport, it was 6:15. I sighed in relief and walked towards the gate with his coffee.

I waited there. I called him, and his phone went to voicemail. Five minutes passed! Was he stuck in traffic? Ten minutes passed! Now, I was starting to panic.

Where was he? His flight was in half an hour. I tried calling his parents, but the same thing happened.

'Claire?' I heard a familiar voice. I looked to my left.

'Thank god!' I sighed. 'Ian, where is Nex?' I asked. His face looked like he'd just witnessed a ghost.

'Nex—he... it's too late, Claire. He left an hour ago. His flight was at 6.' The coffee cup slipped out of my hand.

'What? He said his flight was at 7 p.m. You're pranking me, right? Ian, this isn't funny.' I chuckled while tears started rolling down my cheeks.

'I'm not. His flight left an hour ago. He lied to you.' Of course, he did! My phone chimed with his name.

**Open your glove compartment.**

I ran toward the parking lot and immediately opened the glove compartment. An envelope was resting in there. I took out the letter and read.

*Hi sweetheart.*

*I've left by the time you read this. Please don't hate me. Okay, hate me, but also love me. I know you feel betrayed, but this is for the best. Claire, I could never break up with you, not in my wildest dreams. What we have, it's entirely ours, but the breakup would've changed it. And long distance could ruin it. I don't know if what I did was right or not, but at least by doing this, I will always have your good memories. In the future, if we ever meet again, you can drown me in the lake for doing this to you but if we don't, then please, remember me as a part of your good memories. You're allowed to date anyone. I won't mind because what we had was precious, beautiful, and typical cliche. I love you, Claire, and you're the best.*

*Love, Nex.*

I sobbed. I screamed. I wept. I crumpled the letter and cried.

It was hurting me. Something broke in me as I tried calling him again, but the call didn't connect.

This was worse than a breakup. This fucking closure from Nex ripped my heart open to bleed.

With all our good memories, this one memory will always be bittersweet.

The end of my high school love.

13.

## The Promise

S. R. Behera

Every night,

Looking at the stars high in the sky

I promised myself that in due time,

I will change myself…

To a fierce, mighty one;

Who would never fall for anyone or in anyone's trap.

I will always cherish—what I got and have

and would show all those people

over there who were once laughing at me for my innocence.

14.

## The Day has Finally Come To an End

S. R. Behera

The day has finally come to an end.

End of all those joyous moments

lived back in those immature periods of our life.

End of trusting somebody with our darkest,

scariest, and humiliating secrets condemned by our immature selves.

End of believing the belief... that we are loved by others when it's just a coat covered over the true lies.

End of trust that we imply on others when in reality, it's just a way of assurance,

that others will accept all our faults with warm, open arms.

I guess the day has finally come to an end.

An end where we are frightened of ourselves and what we have become.

The preaching preached by those who think of themselves as profound preachers have influenced our minds and soul.

We believe in what others believe, neglecting the actual truth.

We are scared of being a loner,

We are scared of being judged, criticised for showcasing or talking about our pains,

We are failing as humans.

We are failing from being ourselves…

The day has finally come to an end.

15.

# The Last Period

Arjun Unnikrishnan

Long, long ago, when going to school was the normal…

We all cherish that one day, the one where we don't wear formals

The one day where all the periods seem to fly by.

You go to lunch with happiness and joy, as high as the sky.

The world seems to be nothing to you, extremely nonchalant.

It is now time; time to show your hidden talent.

Highest of high spirits, so much that a pair of wings would make you a fairy.

So much pure, unlimited joy, it's a bit scary

For so long, life hasn't been so pleasant

Your face sparks up, much like the moon in her crescent

On the way back to class, you constantly smile and glance at your shoes, knowing that you will change it.

You peek at yourself in the mirror, your eyes brazenly lit

After walking quite a distance, you stop, drink everything in, and take a soft, deep breath

This feeling you will cherish forever, till your very death.

Reality closes in, happiness shrouds all pain,

a lifetime isn't enough to take it all.

You tighten your laces, prevent your heart from flying, and look at that size 5 white football.

This feeling is bliss, something out of this world.

My love and affection for this sport and the joy it gives me will never be in dearth.

16.

# Farewell To My Haven

Yashvi Bulani

A scream tore through the air, and every hand froze. Every eye witnessed the downfall of our respected principal sir as he fell from the top floor of our school, right to the ground, with a proud smile.

Well, his portrait fell, but still.

The smack I planted on my forehead echoed, and the commotion broke through the air.

Our principal was a very humble and an anti-misogynist man. Note the sarcasm. Actually, he was the sheer definition of misogyny. I don't think I have ever had a stronger sense of dislike for anybody else but him.

My puffy, forest-green eyes ached as I tried to make sense of even one person out of the ones running around on our campus like beheaded chickens. Today was our last day on campus; today was our graduation party. And our school was gracious enough to let us do the preparations for it ourselves, on the same day it was to take place. *Geez, why so early?*

The junior art students were having a freak-out party over the portrait in the middle of the horse race of plugging decorations, at whatever corner any horse—student—could find appropriate or empty for that matter. Apparently, our dear principal sir would be very disappointed if he were to not find his portrait at the top of the school's building. His own very prized possession, made by his favourite art students who respected him very much.

A giggle floated to my ears, and I turned around to find Aarav leaning against a classroom wall while a junior shamelessly laughed at every word he let out of his mouth, boosting his already Canada-sized ego.

Aarav and I had been best friends since the third grade. Coincidentally, he was leaning outside our third-grade classroom, making me peek into that one corner of it that I was punished to sit at all those years ago for coming in five minutes late. Aarav had been a back bencher since the start, and the hate I had for him that one hour I was forced to sit beside him was endless; he'd chatted my brain away. It was finally then when I cursed him flimsy that he shut up and looked at me wide eyed.

I taught him every curse present in my limited vocabulary back then, and we instantly couldn't live without each other. It was lame, but I wouldn't change a thing. Except everything was going to change after today.

It already had.

The anticipation that had rolled off the walls of my school, my second home, had now disappeared. There were no dusty footprints on the floors of our corridor. All was now scrubbed away neatly, and I was forgotten. We, the class of 2022, were forgotten. It was like we had never put our tiny third grade feet there, and as we ran through the hallway, chasing one another after our lunch period, we were already in twelfth grade.

All the times that we sneaked out of our classes with a giddy hope of seeing that one person we had been secretly crushing over for two years, the traces of that puppy love were now gone. Though school gave us hell, we found our heaven in our friendships. After a long festive break, our footsteps rushed through the chaotic 9 a.m. corridor and into the classroom in hopes of not missing out the first fifteen minutes with our friends before the teacher finally decided to show up. Those footsteps would never return. In a way, we had left a part of ourselves in those classrooms.

Anyway, back to the point. Back to *Mr I have some urgent work.*

'Aarav!'

He shot off the wall in a millisecond, turning towards my voice with panic swimming in his eyes.

'This is your urgent work? Stop flirting with her. Her mom already hates you!' For understandable reasons, I wouldn't want my daughter around Aarav either, but it was actually her daughter who kept latching onto him after that one game of childish truth and dare in freaking sixth grade.

The junior scurried down the hall, and Aarav turned to me. 'Come on, Sonya! You want me to die alone?'

'If you don't go and help out with the final touches, you *will* die alone. Today itself,' I deadpanned, then sniffled.

Oh god, I couldn't seem to stop. I looked at the wall covered in ant-sized scribbles from who knows whom. We all had scribbled our hearts away on every clean wall we could find. There were ship names for our favourite teachers, our own names written with our crushes in heart bubbles. Talk about cheesy.

Aarav's eyes widened yet again. 'Sonya, darling, I'm not actually going to marry that girl, so don't cry for me just yet; you look like the sky has cracked over your head,' he teased, in an attempt to lighten up the mood, but what happened next made my blood run cold. I wiped my cheek, only to realise it was not my tear that had fallen but the sky, which had cracked open.

My eyes, now wide like saucers, met Aarav's, who mirrored my expression. 'Shit.'

We both turned around to find the commotion still going on,

only now redoubled. Everyone rushed inside the building, dropping whatever they had in their hands. I clenched my palms shut and gritted my teeth. It was not even close to monsoon season, so how? Why me? Why us?

I'd been dreaming about this iconic day for years, and though it was already not going as planned, not even close, did this have to happen today?

I didn't know what looked sadder—the faces of my classmates and me, or the Principal's portrait now lying drenched in water beside the ruined Rangoli.

An arm slung over my neck, turning me halfway around, and Razia's grinning face came straight into view. 'Come with me.'

I was bewildered over how she could be smiling at a time like this, but then again, she had always been a bit of an optimist, if not a lot. I noticed that all the students were following us to wherever Razia was leading.

We entered our cafeteria, and the sight soared my heart. It was packed in there, and chaos had swallowed the air. All of my remaining classmates and school staff were spread across the room, happily enjoying our cafeteria's food. Razia dragged me forward to our friends who, like me, looked very much hungover on tears but were now together and happily chatting our last day of childhood away.

Two of my other friends engulfed me in a hug, and a nostalgic feeling washed over me. All the laughter we had shared under this one roof, the friendship and mistakes we had made, the conspiracies, the jokes, the tears, the complains we had, the cafeteria's food, and our teachers echoed through me.

As I laughed when a bite of the most delicious food—not really—was shoved in my mouth, I saw some of our teachers laughing joyously at us, and our principal suddenly smiled, neither of those two things seemed bad. In fact, I knew I'd crave them for the rest of my life.

So I tried, I tried, and bottled up all of that joy inside me of that last day in my haven.

17.

# The Beginning of Us

Tiyasa Tikadar

I wished for the earth to swallow me.

I kept my eyes on the ground and my hands clasped behind my back, well aware of the 20 pairs of eyes on me in the music room. My entire face was red and on fire, for embarrassment or for being the centre of attention, that I didn't know.

'You'll never be successful as a writer if you keep writing horrible things like this!' My English teacher almost yelled at me, making me flinch. How did I even get myself into this situation?

Oh wait, I knew the answer. I wrote a novella about a seventeen-year-old girl being abused by her stepfather and how her guy best friend tried to protect her from him. I knew, the book was a little bit messed up, but it was all fiction. Damn it, I even wrote 'everything in this book is entirely fictional' at the beginning.

Well, apart from the characters.

Instead of making my own characters, I decided to use real life people as my characters and didn't even bother to ask those people if I could use them as fictional characters in my book. But that day, I'd decided that I'd change the name of my characters when I'd go home. And I would've had it if it hadn't been for that asshat of my classmate, AJ, who practically snatched the manuscript from me and showed it to our English teacher, Miss Collins.

The horror!

Not going to lie, I lowkey expected her to praise me for my writing. I mean, my readers on Wattpad—an online writing platform—did claim that they loved my writing. But she didn't. Instead, she yelled at me for writing "such utter bullshit", using real life characters and all.

'Look at me, Jui!' Miss Collins yelled again. I slowly raised my head and met her dark eyes with my light brown ones. She didn't react to my glassy eyes. In fact, her eyes grew angrier, and she seemed livid.

'Don't you dare weep like a baby,' she seethed and crumpled my manuscript in her hands. It felt like my heart stopped beating when I realised what she was about to do.

*Please don't. Please don't. Please don't.*

But she did. She did anyway. She crumpled my manuscript and threw it away, right inside the bin nearest to us. I could hear a few gasps around me. That was when I let a tear escape.

I'd worked so hard on that story. So freaking hard and she decided to throw it away like a freaking tissue paper?

Rage filled my entire body as I fisted my hands and kept my eyes on her. I'd have done something very wrong to her, had she not been my teacher.

She folded her arms across her chest and said, 'Next time, don't write something like that. I'll not tolerate this kind of behaviour in my class.' This kind of behaviour? As if I was writing that for my exams. 'Now go to your classroom and away from my sight. Go!'

I kept my head down and tried my best not to cry. Without saying anything, I walked out of the classroom. And only then did I let my tears fall.

**Lunch break**

'I hate her,' said Annie, my best friend, once she heard the recap of the incident that happened in the music room. 'Teachers are supposed to encourage their students, not discourage them.'

I let out a sigh. 'Can we please stop talking about this?'

Annie grumbled but didn't comment any further.

'What are you going to do now?' Preeta, my other best friend, asked.

I shrugged, not bothering to give her a reply, and stared at my unopened lunch box.

The truth was, even I didn't know what I was supposed to do. While working on that book, I was uploading chapters on Wattpad as well. But the manuscript was almost done while barely half was done on Wattpad. And now, I didn't have anything to post there. I had to rewrite the entire story once again.

I was so invested in my own thoughts that I didn't notice someone was standing behind me until they opened their mouth.

'Mind if I talk to you for a second?' A smooth but deep voice came from behind me.

I inhaled sharply when I heard that guy and turned around to look at him.

*Oh, my—*

The first thing I noticed was his eyes. Crystal blue. Then his eyebrows and eyelashes. Dark like a forest and so long that it touched his cheeks. Then his lips. Plump and pretty pink. And very kissable. Then I roamed my eyes over his face and noticed that his cheekbones as well as his jaw were so sharp that it could cut glass. My eyes fell on strands of dirty blonde falling over his forehead. And that was when the thought struck me.

He was not from India.

I'd heard from Preeta that an American student had joined our school for the next two semesters and that he was attractive and had got himself a fan club in just a few days.

She didn't tell me he was this attractive, though.

Realising he was standing there, waiting for us to say something, I opened my mouth.

'What?' I said breathily.

He cracked a grin, and God, I almost passed away then and there. How could someone be so freaking gorgeous?!

'Could I talk to you for a few seconds?' he asked again, this time a little bit slower.

'Yeah, sure,' I said, as if I was out of breath.

He held out his hand. 'Austin. Austin Miller.'

I shook his hand with mine. He had a nice grip. 'Jui Mazumdar.'

He stuffed his hands into his pant pockets and looked right into my eyes. Time stood still as Austin and I continued to stare at each other. The more I stared into his eyes, the clearer his orbs seemed to get.

There was something intense about his eyes. It felt like he was staring right into my soul when he was looking at me with pretty eyes.

'So,' I broke the silent atmosphere. 'You want something? From me?'

He cocked his head and smiled lightly. 'I was wondering if you'll be available after school or not.'

'Huh?' I asked, confused.

'After school. Will you be free after school? I have something important to show you.'

With knitted eyebrows and confusion filled eyes, I said, 'Me? But we just met.'

A lazy smile played on his lips as he said, 'I believe that

"something important" is yours, Jui.'

Heat rose to my cheeks. My name never sounded so good from anyone's lips. God, I hoped he wouldn't notice my blush.

'I swear I'm not going to kidnap you,' he added. 'I'll just give you your thing and go away.'

'What thing?'

He winked at me. 'That's for you to find out.'

And with that, he walked away from me and towards the group of boys he was friends with.

I turned to look at Annie, who was looking at me as if I were some real-life princess in disguise.

'What the hell was that?' She all but squeaked, gaining a little attention from the people around us.

'Tone it down!' I whisper-yelled at her. 'And I don't know what just happened.'

'Will you meet him? After school?' she asked, her eyes still as wide as saucers.

I shrugged, looking back at where he was standing and laughing with his friends.

'Maybe.'

******

I was panting by the time I reached Austin.

'You didn't tell me where to meet you, idiot,' I panted out.

I thought he was going to meet me behind the old store in front of our school. Or near the garden beside the elementary school.

Who knew that idiot was going to meet me at the bus stand?

He raised an eyebrow. 'I thought you'd guess it right.'

'But I didn't.' I snapped and winced at my own tone. 'Sorry, I didn't mean to snap at you.'

I thought he would be offended by my harsh tone, but instead, he seemed amused.

I narrowed my eyes at him. 'What's that thing you were talking about?'

Greek God or not, I still didn't fully trust him. He was a stranger to me, and a part of me believed he was going to pull some prank on me.

Every doubtful thought disappeared when he held out a stack of papers in his hands.

'Here.'

I drew my eyebrows together. 'What's that?'

He sighed, then took my hand and placed that stack of papers on my hand. 'Check it out yourself.'

I looked at him weirdly before I took my gaze to the papers in my hands.

A gasp tore from my lips the moment I scanned over the first paper.

What the—

I moved to the next one, and then the next, and finally, after going through the first 5 pages of the stack, I looked back at Austin with wide eyes.

'How did—how do you—what?' I couldn't form any sentences.

His intense eyes softened as he said, 'I found your manuscript in the dustbin.'

I looked back at the papers. 'But this is clean. Not crumpled.' I took my gaze back at him. 'And the handwriting is not mine.'

I had a messy handwriting while the one in these papers was clean.

He rubbed the back of his head rather awkwardly. 'Well, that original manuscript of yours was not in a good condition.' He shuddered. 'And it smelled nasty. So I copied the entire thing down on a new paper.'

Shock filled my mind. 'You copied the entire thing down?!' I asked in disbelief. 'You don't even know me properly. And how did you know about this?'

He crossed his arms over his broad chest. 'I was in the music room when the incident happened.'

'But I didn't—'

'But you didn't notice me because you were too busy trying not to strangle Miss Collins. Though it would have been a lot of fun if you did.'

'Shut up,' I grumbled.

The corner of his lips quivered in amusement. 'And to answer your last question, I know a lot about you.'

'Were you stalking me?' I tried to make a joke, though a part of me wondered if he indeed was a stalker or not.

He let out a low chuckle. 'No, I wasn't.' He looked into my eyes as he continued, 'Over thirteen thousand followers on Wattpad, almost a million reads on your first story, "Love Me or Hate Me" and exactly three thousand and fifteen followers on Instagram. Am I right?'

'I thought you were not stalking me,' I said as I stared at him in disbelief, once again. 'And how do you know about all this stuff?'

I mean, even my parents weren't aware of these.

'I wasn't. I just have a photographic memory.' He pointed at his head.

'Answer my last question,' I demanded like a terrified girl who was about to be gutted.

'About that,' he drawled out as he stepped a foot closer to me until we were just a few inches apart from touching each other. He stared down at me as he continued, 'You'll have to find it out yourself. And for the umpteenth time, I am not stalking you. At all.'

Something about him made me trust him. Also, he didn't give that kind of aura at all.

'Sorry. I have trust issues,' I told him softly and honestly.

'It's alright.' He shrugged and adjusted his black backpack. Giving a curt nod, he said, 'See ya tomorrow.' With that, he turned on his heels and started walking away from me.

'Wait!' I called out, though I had no idea why.

He turned back around with a raised eyebrow, silently asking, 'What?'

'Um, thank you. For wasting your time on this.' I pointed to the manuscript in my hand. 'It wasn't necessary, but this really means a lot to me.' I thanked him genuinely, since that was the least I could do for someone who spent their entire time copying my crumpled and nasty manuscript.

He smirked and yelled, 'Tomorrow 10 a.m. at Park Café. Wear something casual.'

'What?' I yelled back in confusion.

'I'll answer your last question if you decide to hang out with me tomorrow.' He smiled goofily at me and added, 'It's a date, sweetheart!'

My face was on fire when he yelled out the last part. Thank God barely anyone was there.

I bit my lower lip to stop myself from smiling like an idiot. I shook my head at what, that I didn't know.

'That's a no?' He asked.

Holding my new and fresh manuscript closer to my chest, I yelled out, 'Meet you tomorrow, Austin!'

He smiled a big smile, and I almost swooned over it.

Later on, I found out that he was actually one of my OG readers, and that's how he knew so much about me.

And that was the beginning of our story.

The story of Jui, a writer, and Austin, her favourite reader.

18.

# The Storm

Jash Chauhan

When the storm was passing, you held it tight,

knowing that it was not the end.

But you made yourself believe it was all right.

After some time, things turned fine

With cold winds passing and some sunshine.

With every time, you see yourself heal, so that now again, you won't let it feel.

But the law of nature nobody can understand,

you feel a spark like your feet touching hot sand.

Of all the last things, this feels so good,
that spark you let changes your mood.

You reach cloud nine
Believing things turned fine and praying to God for this lovely time.

But this was another storm passing by, to make you strong and so dry
This shall too just pass, just the time is high
Just let it flow and don't question why.

19.

## Best Days

Jash Chauhan

I sat down today with a pen and book
to write about my school, the days of that time,
and some faces started to appear that I used to call mine.

I shared a seat with a friend called Heni,
a wonderful and funny one in many.
We thought of starting a business after school like the children always do,
but after the time passed and so did the years,
still, we laugh at the idea we had thought
which slowly disappeared.

Also, there was a day when
I was bashed by my class teacher for standing like him
and for his pose I tried,
That day, all I did was laugh and cry.

And to her, whom I liked and cared
To stand in front of and look into her eyes
Was still a dare.

I saw shy and kept to myself
Like the world at bay.
Still, I think for all the faces I knew and also do pray.

We promised each other to stay in touch.
We are still deciding when to meet for lunch.

To each one of you, whom I missed on this day today, I have lived a time together.
That alone will be my best moment with you all forever.

20.

## High School Love

Krish Malhotra

You're the reason I am single,

You're the reason I don't need to be in a relationship.

But now that I think about it,

Maybe shake some things about it

Broke up in the second,

Came running back with all my fears.

But maybe you are the one,

Maybe you need someone.

But that's not me,

'Cause I am broke,

I am hurt,

I am exhausted and fed up.

Sometimes when I think about it

Maybe you're the one,

Not for me but someone else.

21.

# Frenemies

Ananya Barman

'You look like a blood-sucking monster,' I commented as I watched my best friend, Natasha, wolf down spaghetti with tomato sauce gliding from the corner of her bottom lips to her soft chin.

We were sitting at our usual favourite snack bar in the city, some miles away from where we stayed. I was rambling about something which no one was actually paying attention to. My stupid girlfriends were busy reading memes on their phones or giggling over something or the other, and the monster who listened to me sometimes was busy with her date—yes, yes, I mean her plate!

Tomorrow was our school. It was the most prestigious private school in Scotland. Though exclusive, it also had that typical high school setting like other high schools. There were swaggers, popular kids, bullies, nerds, Romeo-Juliets, and finally, drama-queen gossip girls.

Thinking about school always made me sick and take me back to when I used to be an introvert in my previous grades, sitting in a corner, staring at one book when I was actually not reading, because I wanted to stay in my comfort zone. But now that my classmates had succeeded in making me one of those characters in a horror comic book, I wouldn't lie, I enjoyed going to school now. From loving peace to breaking peace, I grew up! But still, the fact that I needed to wake up at the crack of dawn every day for school gave me panic attacks.

After returning from the snack bar, Natasha fell on her flat ass, and her reality wrapped. Though she was a couch potato like me for most of the day, she seemed to get some supernatural power in the morning. She became so active that she almost always got both our breakfast and dishes done on time. On the other hand, there was not even one day when I woke up without an alarm clock and Natasha yelling at me. Getting ready at the right time for school was not just my cup of tea, so I gave up on that idea long back.

**The next day**

*'Beep-beep-beep…'*

'Wake up bitch! We'll be late for school,' Natasha howled.

'I'm up!' I sat up indolently, my eyes half open and craving those last five minutes of extra sleep which always ended up as another fifty minutes.

I was feeling too lazy to stand up, so I crawled my way to the washroom.

Today, instead of the usual miscellany of pieces of denim, crop tops, and oversized jackets, I went for something different. But you know what was I wearing? A solid shirt with formal trousers because I wanted to look obedient in class for the remaining few days that were left before our last day in school.

Natasha and I reached school on time, fortunately, and straightened our backs for the day. But as soon as I was about to enter the class, I bumped into a tall, lanky boy with green eyes, caramel skin, and short, brown, messy hair. It was none other than my frenemy, Aiden.

'Can't you see and walk?' he commented. Normally, I cringed at his words, but today, my head and heart disagreed to do so. Tilting his head a little, confusion evident on his face, arms crossed over his chest, he waited for a savage reply like always, but I didn't say anything.

I settled down at the backbench, thrashing my bag at something but soon realised that it was not an object but Natasha.

After teasing Natasha a little, finally, it was our maths class, and she was happy to sit next to the window, so she could see the clouds and reroute her attention from maths. It had always been her least favourite subject.

All the classes went pretty well, and finally, it was our lunch break, when a group of nine, ten gathered around one tiffin box full of noodles or some other delicious food. One spoon always failed as twenty fingers took over.

After we finished gulping down like vultures, I felt someone bumping my seat. I turned around to look who it was and frowned at the face that just appeared. 'You again?' I questioned and the brown-haired boy chuckled.

'Sorry, Fiona, I wanted to apologise for my prank from earlier in person.' Aiden said and went with his hand through his smooth hair.

'First of all, I don't accept apologies from you, and what prank? That was such kiddish behaviour, the joke's on you,' I said, and he started laughing hard.

'It was a kiddish prank for a kiddish girl.' He smirked and leaned closer to me, making me blush a little. 'I love playing pranks on you, little girl,' he said and went back to his seat.

'You're impossible,' I said and turned back, leaving him with a smirk on his face.

## After 4 months

It was the night before the farewell day, and I couldn't sleep all night because my brain wouldn't turn off, and there were so many things on my mind, ranging from all the school memories, bad and good, to Aiden. I never thought I would fall for him and that he would be my first crush. If someone were to say I was "in love", Aiden would be the last person, but now, I couldn't stop thinking about him after that day.

So, we had talked, laughed, fought, and traded remarks during class. That was most of our communication. But that day was a bit different. That was the first time when a thing like this was happening to me. I was happy for no reason whenever Aiden's thoughts came into my mind. My heart did a pirouette whenever I saw him at school, and I was so jealous of Becky when she used to sit with him in class. Every small thing about him was affecting me. I knew he already knew about me like everyone else in school, but I wanted him to see me differently.

I could find my situation fit perfectly in a Hindi romantic song when Natasha used to explain to me the lyrics as she is an Indian and obsessed with Bollywood. One song was something like *"Dil yeh mera bas mein nahin"*, which meant "My heart is not in my control", and yes, that was exactly what was happening to me right now.

Finally, our farewell day came, and I was sitting among a pile of clothes. I was like every other woman who had nothing to wear (although I was happy about wearing Natasha's black slit skirt with a white vest top after fighting with her for it).

We reached school on time, and today, the bag felt a little heavier—not because of the books, but because today, it carried endless memories. Students in the first benches made notes, but we backbenchers made memories; maybe that's why, the subdued feeling was not sinking in. Smiling faintly, I entered our classroom. Everyone was called one by one by our homeroom teacher to give a farewell speech.

Hormones rushed through my body as I heard the teacher call out Aiden's name. He was wearing black pants, and a black shirt with folded sleeves exposing his veins which were adequate to drive me crazy. My heart was racing fast than a racing car. I wanted to keep my feelings hidden for as long as humanely possible, but I could feel my cheeks burning. I had been debating with myself whether I should confess to him or not for the past two weeks but was unable to gather the courage.

'Let's go,' Natasha dragged me by the arm to Aiden, and I had no choice but follow her obediently, or else her unpredictable mouth would divulge everything to him in front of everyone. The moment he stood in front of me, my hair moved with the wind, and my limbs, at the same time, relaxed. There was like no ground below my feet. Only a canyon of dark black darkness surrounded me, and I could see no one around me except his handsome face. I was not afraid; it felt nice to be with him.

'Dude, what the fuck?' Natasha hissed, accompanied by my other friends rolling their eyes at me. Aiden's dark green eyes fixated on mine like he was searching for depth. He was not sure what was happening and why I was panicking, but he remained patient.

Confusion and anxiety battled within me. I got down on my knees, and the three golden words slipped through my mouth. 'I love you.' I paused, and my heart swelled. I couldn't look up and see his face. Suddenly, I felt Aiden's warm hands tighten around mine, and I smiled looking up at him.

'I love you, too,' he said, putting his bag down and taking my waist. Butterflies exploded in my stomach at his touch, setting my whole body on fire.

'Aww,' someone purred from beside me and we two blushed.

Our beautiful high school journey ended, giving rise to a new one.

22.

# Days to Relive

Anwesha Banerjee

Vinita barged into her room, banged the bedroom door open, threw her backpack on the floor, and flumped back on the bed, leaving a deep sigh.

Hot tears cascaded down her cheeks, wetting the bedsheet and reddening her large, almond shaped eyes. She blew her nose into a hankie, curled into a semi-circle, and whimpered nonstop as the day's events played at the back of her head.

'Why did he give the flower to Arpita? He didn't have to do it, right?' she reasoned.

'But why do I care suddenly? Argh! He's eating my head!'

Vinita couldn't decipher the odd reasons. Hell! She was having a tough time decoding her weird thought processes recently.

Things were changing pretty fast and quite rapidly. Her best friend, the boy who stood some inches short and came up to her ears, had sported a growth spurt in the past eighteen months and now towered over her. The same weakling whom she was used to slapping and kicking hijacked her brain, something she didn't intend.

'How come things which were as simple as A, B, C, D appear this complicated now! What do I even see in that idiot?'

Thinking of which, Vinita was quite a good student. This was the third year she was chosen as the head girl and was the captain of the girls' debate team which had bagged a gold in the National Interschool Debate Competition in 2018. She was smart and intelligent, but worst of all… a tomboy!

'Pathetic! Did I just curse myself?'

Vinita gasped.

Covering her mouth, she exhaled. Yes, she was getting more and more pathetic day by day, and it started exactly when…

The year was 2016. Vinita and Sumit were both fresh off their tenth board exams and theirs being a typical Indian family, theirs was a month of respite after a year of constant studying and persistent nit-picking by concerned parents. The roadside Momo seller was stalled as usual, and like a cart on wheels, they had gravitated towards those soft, stuffed dumplings that came with a bowl of flavourful soup and fiery sauce on the side.

People would assume Sumit to be the hero in the story. They might deduce him to be a poor girl's saviour. But no; here, the case was the exact opposite. Or how else could you fathom a sickly, stunted teenager escaping the wrath of muscular, growing boys with the strength of elephants and aggressiveness of horny male lions?

The answer was simple. It was Vinita, the hijra. Well, that was what the boys called her.

'Woohoo, look who's here? The frog and his princess!' A shrill voice which sounded close to a broken banshee came from a distance, followed by an obnoxious wolf whistle.

Sumit and Vinita gorged on their plates, unperturbed by their taunting. With time, they had grown used to it.

'Hey, didn't you hear us, dipshit?' another hollered. 'Yeah, our eunuch is probably going to protect her lost puppy, isn't she?' the taunting grew.

Vinita balled her hands into fists.

'Vini, please don't fight. Let us go. Come.' He pulled at her arm, his sweaty palms speaking of the tension.

Would she leave without a fitting reply? No.

She jerked away. Clenching her jaws, she said, 'When will you cease to be a sissy?'

Being the timid idiot, Sumit bowed his head and stood still, helpless as a kitten. 'I know I'm worthless,' he whimpered.

'Shut up! Grow some balls, will you? Or else these chipmunks will forever take chances!'

Vinita stationed her plate on the stall owner's cart and rolled her sweatshirt sleeves up. It was time to put those old karate lessons to good use. 'Hey, langurs! Want to see the other side of the coin?'

Within minutes, two boys lay flat on the ground, crouching in pain, while the third had fled the scene even before it started.

Limping, she had been supported home by Sumit, who had volunteered to offer first-aid. The way he gently dabbed the antiseptic on her bruised knee, blowing air at it to reduce the irritation, the way he softly handled those multiple scratches and cuts, constantly complaining about her boorishness, although aware she was capable of tackling much more!

It was at that time that she found...

A series of consecutive rings broke her reverie. Wiping away the dried tears, Vinita answered.

'Vini, can you help me with a sum?'

Red with rage, she gritted her teeth and barked, 'May I know why the first boy wants my help? Where is your girlfriend? Shouldn't she be the one helping you?'

'What? She isn't my girlfriend! I just—'

'Yeah, yeah, whatever. As if I care!' She rolled her eyes. 'And no,

I won't be able to—'

'Wait, wait. Are you crying by any chance?' he questioned.

*Curious cat! Now he can what, mind read?*

'No, idiot! I'm not! And why should I?'

'No… I mean... your voice… I just know when you're crying. Are you this vexed because I gave her the flower?' There was a slight hint of tease in that tone. 'It was just a bloody dare, stupid!' he jested.

'And—and you… you just agreed?! Just like that! I thought you were—' She jerked to a stop. *Oh my God! What am I saying? She thought to herself. The idiot's probably grinning like a Cheshire cat! What the hell is wrong with me? Why am I behaving like a nincompoop?*

And as she surmised, laughter boomed from the other end of the line. 'And you thought I was, what?' he chortled. 'Well, are you jealous by any chance or just plain missing me since I have shifted?'

Vinita clenched her teeth, anger rising as she dissected his brain with a compass within her mind. Given a chance, she wouldn't hesitate to give him a blue eye, though it was doubtful whether it could be that easy. No more the creeper, he had considerably bulked up and his lean muscles manifested an athletic physique.

'Go and eat shit, you fool!' she cursed and disconnected the line as another string of tears quickly pooled up.

The next day was the last of school.

It was the day of farewell before the dreaded twelfth board exams; a bittersweet moment for all, an end of two years of constant striving amidst late night reads, silent gossip, bulk of assignments, the morning rush, and finally, sweet, guiltless crushes. As Vinita chomped on flaky patties, a swift side eye revealed Sumit leaning against the wall, chatting to a girl who she knew had an inkling towards him. *Doesn't he see that? Is he this oblivious? Or is he into her, too?*

'Argh! These voices!' she screamed.

'What the hell? Did you just start talking to yourself? You were always nuts but now seem to have lost a part of your brain permanently!' Ankit supplied while munching on chocolate chip cookies. 'And wipe those crumbs off your face, will you? It looks gross!' he said and offered his handkerchief. Vinita snatched it away and rubbed her face like a maniac, vexed and agitated at Sumit's cool and relaxed demeanour.

'Jerk, bloody idiot, jackass!' She whispered a series of curses amidst clenched teeth. 'Go to hell, you fool! As if I'll ever talk to you!'

'If you like him that much, go and confess. Though I have serious doubts whether he will accept a proposal from another boy!' he finished, while rubbing his hands on the uniform.

Vinita gasped and stared in bewilderment. A reply, even though at the pit of her throat, failed to manifest itself. She blinked in astonishment, mouth forming a slow 'O'.

'What the hell? What in the world do yo—'

Ankit held his palm up. 'No one has ever considered you a girl, okay? And you know you were never one!'

It was true. She never drafted sob stories like her friends did, and never enacted one. She refused makeup; even thousands of YouTube tutorials had failed; her eyeliner was never done properly, damn her shaking hands! Her lipstick, in the nudest of nude colours, was often smudged, and ninety-nine percent of the time, females wanted her as their bodyguard. Her awkward boyish charm bore a stark contrast to an hourglass shape. Not that it was something she was aware of or did anything to highlight. She had been ignorant of things girls paid astute attention to. And so, it remained until Sumit pointed it out over casual conversations regarding dresses and girly stuff.

Yes, it was amusing how Sumit and her girly conversations fit in one frame, but he was her sole friend, her confidant.

It was a part of Vinita being Vinita; awkward, clumsy, eccentric, hot-headed and a practical fool!

Smart and tough as a nail on the outside, a jumbled mess of emotions on the inside.

Could anyone imagine the hopelessness? Could she be any more pathetic?

As the small farewell drew to a close, cheers rose into the air and mingled with frantic shouts and hollers, words of endearment and encouragement and promises of things to follow. Hugs and tears were shared as much as cakes and cookies, patties and pastries, and lots of wishes for the upcoming boards that loomed over them like a sinister death eater. Sumit had not once spoken to her. He had been thoroughly busy gorging on handmade cakes from his female fans; those typical, whiny models who fluttered their eyelashes like barbie dolls at the slightest discomfort.

Disgruntled, Vinita made her way through an empty corridor towards the toilet. The laboratories were barren with chemical bottles and Bunsen burners. Anger and a feeling she couldn't quite articulate, coursed through every nerve of her being. She hated crying like a sissy, but why the hell couldn't those tears be helped?

A quick tug, a hand on her mouth, a door being opened, and the next minute, she found gooey cream smothered all over her face.

'What the f—' she attempted to scream, but large, calloused palms suppressed it. Irate and inflamed, she threw a solid punch, but the guy bent down to avoid it in the neck of time. Furious, she raged like a bull and attempted to immobilise him with a kick to the knee, but her efforts were neutralised again, and she found herself enmeshed within muscular, strong arms. Flustered and peeved, she writhed and squirmed, but strategic blocks rendered her efforts futile.

'Someone seems to be awfully displeased, doesn't she?' His hot breath fanned the curly, unruly tendrils behind her ears. They awakened strange, queer sensations while she felt his warm palm tighten around her toned stomach.

Her irregular breathing calmed, and breasts rose up and down at a gentler pace, while his hands curved a bit towards her hips, still maintaining distinct decency. Alert and aware, an alarm rang within her mind, but she was too entranced to react. Those feelings were foreign to a whole new level.

He turned her around and simultaneously pulled her towards himself. Holding her waist with one hand, he stared deep into her eyes, scooped a portion of strawberry cream from her plump lips, licked it off his fingers, and inserted a note into her skirt pocket. Then, he left as quickly as they had entered.

Vinita was so dazed and startled that the thought to vacate the room at that very instant totally evaporated off her head.

It wasn't at least an hour later while she was returning home by bus that she opened the crumpled piece of paper.

*'I love your short, broken nails as much as I adore your chopped, curly hair. Your awkward gestures fascinate me. I love the eccentricity in you. In short, I love you, Vini. I always have.*

*P.S. That was an indirect kiss.*

*Yours,*

*S.'*

23.

# The One I Wish

Kriti Mohanty

You are like glittering moonlight
above the moving sea at night.
You are like the fresh summer breeze
that swept me off my feet.
I always wondered if you were real
and you were always with me saying, 'Yes, dear.'
With that smug smile
and those sweet eyes.
You held my heart from the very first sight.
No matter how many seconds, minutes, or hours we spent,
it was you that made my feelings crescent.
It was a big deal then, and so it is now.
I don't care if we are mad,
when all I want is to talk it out.

## *The One I Wish*

They say you are too good to be true,
but I still hold on to you.
No matter what society says,
there's hope, and so, it's great.
When we don't talk for days, and I fear if it's all okay,
You knock on my door and smile, 'Let's drive away.'
I rush towards every opportunity to be with you.
Because when it's true, I will have moments to hold on to.
And when we think it's all over,
you surprise me with a collision.
The warmest of smiles can melt even the coldest of hearts.
I'll love you on warm summer mornings
and cold winter nights.
I'll freeze the time, and feel the hours,
To let our wild souls bind.
I don't know if you are real or just in my imagination,
but I will love you either way.
I will hold your hand,
even when you are not there.
Because for the one I wish, I will always wait.

24.

## The Darkness

Kriti Mohanty

I think the darkness calls me because I belong there.

I might have done something different

if I want to go there.

Do you think you know better?

But isn't this my life?

If I wish to follow,

who are you to stop me?

You call me to tell me,

'Let's try again tomorrow.'

I know you care

but just let me be.

If I wish, the only one who will go is me.

I will go where my eyes take me.

I will go where I am never wrong.

Never scared, never hurt.

Just me and the vast universe.

And so I know,

The darkness calls me because I belong

forever and ever

That's where I will be gone.

25.

## The Days We...

Kumud Jain

The days we'd fight to play on the ground,
The days where we struggled to pass,
The days we nurtured nature,
The days when rock and scissors wasn't just a game,
The days we had the freedom to talk,
The days we cared to smile,
The days we felt hurt for others,
The days we stood up to wrong,
Those were the days,
My high school days.
Whether good or bad
I lived for those days.

26.

# The Adventures of Dumdum on the Staircase

Halo C

'You sure you want to go to the library?' She asked.

'Yep,' I answered with a childish smile, as I faced her on a staircase.

'Really?' she asked, suspicious of my intentions.

That was one of many conversations I had with my first crush where I simply hid my true feelings from her. As she stood atop me on the staircase every time, she floated in the air, with each step becoming a metallic floor that stood between us on an enchanted castle that remained suspended at mid-air for all of eternity. Did the steps between us on the staircase represent a spatial distance, or was it time itself? No matter how many years passed, she would always be unreachable...

Before she showed me the skies, I simply lived in lands of my own as I deserved no place in the real world. In my metropolis, shopping malls moved about like tracked vehicles, with their internal floors capable of expanding infinitely. Nano drones formed entire pavements of roads at a simple thought, negating the need for concrete. Even the internet was something we could access with our own minds, with neuro links.

I was content with life until one day, despite my ordinariness, fate put me in a world of gifted individuals: the top class.

'Halo, did you watch the biology documentaries?' My teacher, Yee, asked.

Excitedly, I exclaimed, 'No, but I read about how humans' intelligence could be genetically enhanced. What if we use that to cure autism?'

'Nonsense, Halo. Stay back later!'

With that, many in class glanced at me curiously as I attempted to share my innovative approaches to science. 'That sounds interesting…' most replied with avid interest.

I eventually noticed Javelin, who was my classmate in school years before. Javelin had barely changed at all. He was the head prefect; a born leader who had grown slightly distant from me.

'Javelin! Want to go watch a movie after school?' I asked him one Tuesday at a school staircase that led up to the library.

'No thanks… I have a prefect meeting later!' He replied enthusiastically.

I followed him as he ran up to the library for his prefect duties, hoping to join him as I was his friend. But then, she appeared…

'I want to go to the library!' I lied sheepishly for the first time.

The short but attractive prefect on duty, Courts, smiled and rejected me. 'No, you don't!'

Prefects in our school were imparted with glorious responsibilities as they guarded every nook and cranny of the school, including the staircase.

I implored, 'But we're from the same class!'

'Fine! What will you read in the library?'

'Biology books!'

'What topic?'

I stammered, as science to me had no boundaries, and I had not read a single chapter...

'Circuits!'

After a long stare, she giggled, saying: 'That's physics, dumdum…'

Blushing at my foolishness, I ran like I never did before. Clearly, I excelled at the art of lying! With that, a connection was born.

'Look, I drew a city with wings!' I told Erwin one day, the class' friendliest artist, who had won awards for his exquisite drawings.

'Revolutionary!' Erwin replied enthusiastically.

I finally had another friend besides Javelin. I was never as special as they were, but at least I had some quirks that gave me such talented friends! From then, I began sharing my incredible ideas from applications of solid light, self-created game realities and AI powered animals!

Surprisingly, Courts approached us, smiling at my masterpiece. She exclaimed, 'Great job, dumdum, looks like you have other talents besides biology!'

Erwin rolled his eyes as Courts began to ask me more questions about my drawing. Surprisingly, Erwin simply walked away. Perhaps, he wanted to discuss my masterpiece with others! For some reason, Courts was astounded by my ideas even though they were inferior to Erwin's.

The following Tuesday, I went to Courts, who was speaking to Javelin. Her face was crestfallen as Javelin noticed me. Had I become so popular that they were now talking about me?

Eager to partake in their conversation, I ran towards them. Javelin darted away, saying: 'Hey Halo, I have to go do my homework!'

'What's Javelin like?' Courts initiated.

'He's a great person. I've been his best friend for years.'

'Just be careful…' Courts whispered.

'What are you talking about? You look like an ape right now!'

'What?'

'That's right! You look so angry and ugly like that ape I watched, thanks to your weird makeup, on top of clay on your face!'

Courts was bewildered as she recalled our clay art lesson a while ago. She blushed and looked away, saying, 'You're the worst, Halo!'

Still, she eventually laughed, almost mystically…

Things took a turn for the better in my elite class. Besides my two great friends, Javelin and Erwin, I had Courts, whom I spoke to every Tuesday at the staircase. Regardless of how crude my teacher was towards me, I always had Javelin, who spent much time with me, and Erwin, who always believed in my flair. Even nature testified to my unique friendships with them one day.

One day, I broke my arm after plunging into the ground, following a strenuous sports lesson. At least I had friends! My teacher asked the class, 'I need someone I can trust to be Halo's buddy.'

'I'll do it!' My trusty friend, Javelin, answered.

'As expected of the top prefect,' Yee acknowledged.

Courts approached me in class for ironically only the second time despite her fondness for me, asking, 'How's your arm, dumdum?'

'It's good, why didn't you volunteer to be my buddy?'

'C'mon, people think you are the dumbest in class. Of course, I can't hang out with you, right?' Courts replied in pretentious disdain with a wry smile.

'Wow, next time I'll make sure to push you off the stairs and see who accompanies you.'

'I'm smart, you know… I even know who your true enemies are.'

I was slightly perturbed by her statement but laughed it off. Courts shook her head and left me with Javelin.

Seeing her rare act of kindness, Javelin whispered into my ear, 'Do you like Courts?'

Having never even thought of romance in my life, I gasped in disgust initially, before I recalled all my playful moments with the snarky girl. Before I knew it, I nodded in silence. Javelin promised he would keep it a secret.

One day, Yee said: 'Today, each of you will be folding paper mailboxes and putting in your best wishes for whichever friend you want!'

I put in my personalised letters for Javelin and Erwin. Despite my feelings for Courts, I refused to confess so openly. However, it was truly perplexing how I had received no mails from anyone.

One day, Erwin and Courts were speaking beside my paper plane-like mailbox, with the latter carrying a slip of paper in her hands. I wanted to ask them what happened, but Courts left the classroom, while Erwin said: 'It's nothing. Courts thinks your mailbox was superbly well designed!'

I trusted Erwin, so I let it be.

Eventually, we were given a test on spatial ability. As I always indulged in my imagination, it was easy: I simply rotated a few shapes, predicted a few contours, and derived the answers. Surprisingly, I was the top in this test, a lucky feat. I was ecstatic, but it was odd how my friends stared blankly, while only Courts knowingly smiled.

Eventually, Valentine's Day came. It was not a Tuesday, but still, she stood there in her unparalleled grace. I greeted her. It was the first time I was near her since my conversation with Javelin and my arm's recovery.

'What are you doing here? It isn't Tuesday,' I inquired.

'How did you know I come on Tuesdays?' she rebounded.

'A simple deduction,' I answered, knowing my feelings were about to burst.

'Never knew you cared about a girl who looks like an ape.'

'Maybe I noticed because you just look ugly…'

'Really, so it's not because I'm pretty, then…'

'Yep!'

'You really are something, aren't you? Right, how did you do so well for that test?'

'I just twisted the shapes in my head.'

'How have you been at the bottom this whole time?'

Incidentally, romantic music began to play to commemorate Valentine's Day. If there was any movie genre I disliked, it was romance but, in that instance…

'You really blow my mind though if you are so good at twisting shapes, do you know how to twist your feet?' she asked as I looked in befuddlement.

'What do you mean?'

'I mean, you wouldn't happen to know how to dance, would you, dumdum?' she asked, blushing with a smile.

'No, why?'

Courts' hand floated towards mine magically, but I quickly put it in my pockets, questioning: 'What are you doing?' Courts put her hands on my shoulders and whispered into my ears: 'Just dance, dumdum.'

Despite my ignorance towards the performing arts, I had the most romantic dance I believed anyone could have by the staircase. My footwork was unbelievably exquisite as I stepped on her toes. She simply ignored it and put her face near mine as she held my hands. It was the first time we ever made physical contact. It was magical.

With every move we made, the steps on the staircase beneath us liquefied, morphing into clouds made of cotton candy. The sun above us continued gleaming as the ball of fire crystallised into a diamond chandelier, allowing us to absorb its radiance. The skies turned dark purple as we fully entered a dream, bound by nothing in the real world except its romantic music.

From then, I could not imagine a day without Courts. Life without her was a void and almost deceitful. In her absence, Erwin and Javelin's words became inexplicably empty, but I continued trusting them as they were my brothers-in-arms. After all, they were as real as she was, right?

One day, to alleviate my pain, Erwin kindly informed Courts and her friends about my feelings. He even spread this across the student population to unite everyone in supporting our relationship. Yet it was odd how everyone would only giggle and whisper into one another's ears whenever they approached me and Courts.

I also wondered how Erwin came to know my secret as I had only told my long-time trusted friend, Javelin…

Oddly enough, Courts never spoke to me again.

One day, I walked to the staircase and asked her, 'Could I go to the library?'

She stood aside for the first time, permitting me to pass silently. I walked to the library and finally opened my first biology book, wondering what had happened.

After that, I went to the staircase everyday hoping for a word from her, but it was for naught.

I continued following Javelin and Erwin and stared blankly as they laughed to no ends as they spoke about my feelings for Courts, teasing my stupidity, though it was of course just playful banter. I could not understand as Courts looked on in disgust as if she expected me to speak up for myself, but they were my friends, so they surely meant no harm?

As we graduated, no one, including Erwin or Javelin, wished me well for my future, leaving me to wonder what had happened to my life this whole time. Why did no one speak to me despite their love for my quirks? Why did Courts never approach me again, ever since Erwin gracefully revealed my secret?

Before I left, Erwin simply passed me a familiar slip of paper that said, 'Hey, dumdum, I always knew you were special for not trying to look special like everyone else. Thanks for everything.'

Tears inexplicably welled up in my eyes as I walked away from the school that gave me such incredible friends as the pieces of the puzzle finally came together…

Years later, I approached the staircase once again, hoping the stairs would liquefy once again to form the incredible clouds of cotton candy where we had our first dance. I even tried to float as we did in my fantasy, but I simply collapsed as I attempted to defy the physics of reality…

To my shock, all that I stepped on was just pure concrete…

The truth hit just as hard as we never danced. I ran as her hand began to slip into mine, simply because I never felt special.

What's more was that I let Erwin reveal my secret because I thought I never had the right to confess, simply because I never felt special.

I reached out into the skies, hoping her hands would slip into mine once again. But alas, there was no one to reach out to, simply because I never felt special.

Indeed, it was I who tainted our fantasy… The magic ended because of my foolishness.

What was it that repulsed her, I wondered? Was it my understandable naivety? The fact I ran as she offered me the greatest dance one could ever have? Or the fact that I never felt special? It never mattered, as the dance never came to be.

27.

# Dear Maddy

Tiyasa Tikadar

Dear Maddy,

I don't even know why I am writing this letter to begin with. Maybe I am writing this to fill the void of you in my remaining life. Maybe, maybe I am writing this so that you don't forget your best friend. Hell, I wish I knew what I am supposed to write in this freaking letter. I should have planned out everything before writing like you did before you worked on your new book. But I think both of us are known to the fact that I am not much of a planner; instead, I like to live in the moment.

Anyway, I am wearing the same hoodie I wore the day I met you. Do you remember that day?

You were sitting under a tree, wearing an olive-green dress and your favourite charcoal-coloured boots. A notebook—with a picture of One Direction on the cover, to be specific—was laid open on your lap. But you weren't writing anything. You were just staring ahead. There were tears in your vacant sapphire eyes, and your peach painted lips were clamped over the end of your favourite pen. Oh, and your knee was scrapped as well. I, in my gothic kinda outfit, went over to where you were sitting and inquired about your bleeding knee. Apparently, a few high school boys had pushed you down when you were walking to the park. I still remember the rage coursing inside my veins and how much I wanted to hit those idiots. But I didn't. Instead, I asked you if you liked One Direction. You said that it was your favourite boyband. It was mine, too.

And that's how our friendship began.

Over the next five years, we had grown so attached to each other that people would barely see us without each other. Some would find our friendship amazing, some would find it weird, and some would find it "disgusting". Yeps, I am talking about Shelley. She hated our asses because apparently, we were "The Powerful Duo" in King City High. God, they even gave us some nicknames as well.

Though there's one thing you were not aware of.

Even though we were the best of friends, I never looked at you through the eyes of one. You were more than a best friend to me, Mads. More than a best friend. I was attracted to you the moment I lay my cloudy eyes on you. And throughout all those years, I fucking fell for you.

Yes, it was me who'd leave those cute little pastel green notes in your locker every day. It was me who'd leave you a bunch of sunflowers every Valentine's Day.

And it was me who'd mail those handmade ornaments to your house on every birthday of yours. (Yeah, it was among those three things I hid from you).

At first, I thought it would be creepy to do so, but you didn't mind it. Actually, you liked your "secret admirer". You liked the fact that someone liked you enough to send you those gifts, even though there were tons of boys running after you. It made me a little bit jealous that you thought your secret admirer was a boy. But at least, it made my job a lot easier.

Though that didn't stop you from going on dates with someone.

I remember how excited you'd get when it came to dating, how you'd get nervous six hours before the date, how you'd rummage through your wardrobe trying to find "that perfect outfit", and how nervously but happily you'd go to those dates and how'd you gush about them after you came back.

And I also remember how much I hated seeing you with someone who wasn't me.

How much my heart would burn in jealousy every time someone who wasn't me got to kiss those pink lips of yours. And how I'd lie on my bed and cry ugly tears because you'd never love me the way I loved you.

The truth was, I had loved you more than a friend, but you loved me like a best friend.

It wasn't until that summer that I came clean and told you about my sexuality. The fact that I was a lesbian. We were sitting at our favourite spot, the place where we first met. I told you everything, well, minus the part where I fell for you. Instead, I told you that there was a girl I was head over heels for and the fact that she was straight and not into me. You listened to every word pouring from my mouth in silence.

Then you smiled. You freaking smiled and told me you loved me the way I was. You assured me that my sexuality wouldn't harm our friendship and that I should be proud of who I was. I think I cried a little that day. And gave you the tightest hug known to mankind.

After that, everything was fine.

Until it wasn't.

August 25th.

The day you suddenly blacked out at your home. The day you were rushed to the hospital. The day I learnt that you had cancer. The day I found out you hid a hideous truth from me.

The day my entire world shattered.

The doctor said it was your last stage—said that you didn't have much time left—said that if I wanted to say goodbye, then I should do it.

I was paralyzed in shock. And I tried to imagine what it would be like, to live in a world where you and your sweet smile wouldn't be there. And I hated it.

Hated that world where you would not be there by my side. I didn't want to live in it.

But I had to, right? Fate had already made its decision, and no matter how much I'd try, I couldn't change it.

So, I went to your hospital room. Sat on the chair by your bed. And held your fragile hand.

You looked so broken and so fragile at that time, there was no sunshine left inside of you. I asked you what if I had to go to One Direction's concert after their reunion alone. I asked you what if I had to go to Paris alone, the place where we always wanted to go after we turned eighteen. You just smiled and said, 'I want you to do whatever we have decided to do. And I promise you that you'll not be alone. I'll be walking right beside you, Irene.' And you said that in your fragile voice.

I didn't utter a word after that. I just sat in silence. But I still held your hand. It felt like years before I told you that I'd always miss you. That I'll never forget you, and that no one would replace you ever. And I kissed your cheek, my way of saying goodbye to you.

And without waiting for your reply, I left the room. I left the hospital and went home.

You left this world exactly two hours and twenty-nine minutes after I left you.

I didn't cry when my mom informed me. I didn't cry the next day. I didn't even shed a single tear during your funeral, not even when I was told to give a speech. But the moment I was home after the ceremony, I cried. I cried and cried and screamed and trashed my entire room.

I cried because I had lost my favourite person in this world.

I cried because I had lost the girl I was in love with.

And mostly, I cried because I had lost my best friend.

My parents came and tried to comfort me, but I couldn't stop crying. How could I?

After realising I had to live a life where you won't be anymore, how could I not shed tears?

My heart broke when I used to see you going on dates with guys from our school, but my soul fucking shattered the moment I lost you forever.

It's Day 13 since you've been gone. I'm sitting in front of your grave. It's drizzling lightly.

And I know you are sitting right beside me. Because you promised me to be by my side, remember?

I'll never get over my heartbreak. But I'm willing to give love a second chance. I'm willing because I know you'd want me to do so.

But remember one thing, Maddy.

No matter what, no one can replace your place in my heart. No one can.

And I'll keep loving you.

Always and forever.

Love,

Irene

28.

## Psychology of a Teenage Heart

Dhruv Kataria

I know I am just a kid from high school,
who is weeping like a bimbo
But it is only because I hate to lose myself
in order of passing through this limbo...

I hoped that I would be loved,
not based on 'because' but based on 'despite '
Cause everyone told me that's what'd I get if I gave life a good
and tough fight.

No one knows what's right and what my future hails,
But always keep pointing out my cons and say I will certainly fail.

I thought it would get easier with every metre of the height,
But thanks to life, it never made my burden any light.

Expectations are the time bombs which will not spare time to heal,
But it is guaranteed,
that with every second it ticks,
you will lose the emotions you want to feel...

And after all the heights and success you had in sight,
You still have to feel lonely and shitty every passing night.

29.

## Days to Relive

Dhruv Kataria

The moments which just passed,
Gave me the memories that still last.
The friendships that didn't make their way,
But still are the ones which will be taken to the grave.
Those secret love affairs which ended in guilt,
Are the ones that I wish could be rebuilt.

When my eyes were just dreaming,
And every happy ending felt soothing,
When this heart was just pure and woundless,
I had a soul which wasn't such a mess.
When I didn't have any void to fill,
Are the days which I wish I could relive.

30.

# A Visit to Remember

Huda Nadeem

Little black rocks in my shoes,
There's an amalgam of winged scary insects
Humming little circles around the room lights
This is what high schools 'bout.

Oh, all of us smelling like sweat
And sweet misery,
My hair pulled tight into a mandarin, tied off with a band
The sunshine ritualistically adoring my cheeks,
Like a candle to be lit,
This is what high school's 'bout.

On a summer evening,
We lay down in the sweet cold grass,
dreaming of our future
Not knowing what we might face,
just in the moment of awe
We lay, breathless,
with no motive to study.
This is what high school's 'bout.

Looking down the hallways,
Is where you shall be for the next quaternary years
Gossip, coffee, lectures, friends
Is all your life will revolve around.
'Study! Study! Study!'
is all they'll say.

We cry, smile, laugh
all together
Forging memories,
To be looked upon day after day.
Such was high school's bittersweet life.

31.

# High School Crush

Priyanka Reddy

*How did I end up in this situation?* Lisa thought as her eyes scanned her four friends. Charlotte, Aaron, Dylan, and Gwen waited for Lisa to choose. Her eyes settled on the beer bottle at the centre of the table, the mouth pointing at her.

If playing truth and dare with high school friends was a bad idea, then playing it when they were half-drunk was like digging her own grave.

Since high school, all five of them met up every once in a while. Sometimes, it was just a month, and sometimes it would be a year before their next reunion. But they'd agreed to meet at least once a year, and they still followed the ritual.

The first time they had played truth and dare was when they were still in high school. Lisa had chosen a dare, and she had to do a pole dance without a pole. She still remembered how embarrassed she was at that time, but now she laughed about it with her friends.

Lisa chose truth. As she watched Charlotte's lips curl into a smirk, she wondered if she should have chosen dare.

'Name your high school crush, Lisa.' Charlotte's eyes jumped to Aaron, who was sitting next to Lisa. Being Lisa's high school bestie,

Charlotte knew Aaron was Lisa's high school crush, yet she still asked her to tell the truth.

Charlotte also knew that even after all these years, when they all were working in various fields, Lisa always compared her blind dates with Aaron subconsciously, like how they didn't have intense green eyes she could get lost in, and how none of her dates didn't even like cats, while Aaron loved them just like her.

Last time, her roommate, Rebecca, went on a trip, and she had to bring Mimi, her cat, with her for their weekend stay at Aaron's lake house. Mimi had connected with Aaron instantly at their previous meeting, which was almost six months and nine days ago.

This time, she was alone, and she couldn't even escape by coming up with an excuse to check on Mimi. They should have just gone to bed after dinner, but Dylan was so thirsty for alcohol, as if he hadn't drunk in ages. Then he had cleared the dining table and spun the bottle. Gwen had rolled her eyes at, Dylan, her boyfriend, but Lisa didn't miss the way her lips lifted into a smile whenever Gwen shared eye contact with Dylan. Since they both had blond hair, the rest of them called those two a golden couple. Lisa didn't understand how it was so easy for them to be together since high school.

'Yes. Say it,' Lisa heard Aaron squeal. If her heartbeat hadn't increased before, it did now. Gulping, she glared at Charlotte for putting her in such a situation. Charlotte just gave her an encouraging smile. She'd always wanted Lisa to confess her feelings.

At one point, Charlotte was about to break the news to Aaron but held herself back at Lisa's request. Lisa didn't want to complicate things between her and Aaron. They had become great friends before she could confess her feelings. The fear of ruining her connection with Aaron had sealed her lips for over ten years.

'Come on, Lisa. Say it and spin the bottle,' Dylan whined.

Lisa's gaze flickered between Dylan and Gwen. If they could still be a couple after so many fights over the years, maybe she might have a chance with Aaron, too. Maybe she wouldn't lose him as a friend. Maybe Aaron could become more than her high school crush.

Lisa exhaled heavily and looked at Aaron. 'Aaron.' There it was. She had said it out loud.

'Yes,' Aaron said, turning to her. He thought she had called him.

*Shit*! Lisa cursed herself mentally. She took her shot finally. 'It's you, Aaron Baxter. My high school crush.'

Lisa's eyes didn't avert from Aaron's perfect face. She watched his playful expression disappear. Silence fell across the room. Her heart pounded. She knew her heart couldn't take the rejection. Fear and insecurities crawled on her back.

Lisa tore her gaze from Aaron's face and glanced at her other friends, who looked like she had thrown cold water on their faces. 'I guess that's the end of the game.' She gulped and tried her best to smile. 'I'll go to bed. Good night, guys.'

Lisa got up from her chair and turned around to walk upstairs without glancing at Aaron's face. She managed to keep her steps subtle. But once she knew she was out of their view, she sprinted to her room and closed the door behind her.

She'd ruined everything. Lisa knew it. She knew Aaron didn't have any feelings toward her. Still, she went and spilt a truth that could ruin their friendship now.

Lisa paced across her room. She slid her fingers into her hair and pulled the brunette roots in frustration. Everything would be ruined. The trust and friendship she had built over the years. *How could she commit such a mistake?*

A knock landed on her door, startling her. *Don't let it be Aaron, God,* she prayed before she opened the door. But her prayers didn't reach God.

'Can we talk?' Aaron asked. Lisa watched Aaron's hesitation, which broke a tiny piece of her heart. There was never any hesitation between them.

Now that the truth was out, Aaron would try to distance himself from her. The thought itself burned her throat.

'Yes,' Lisa nodded. Aaron led her towards the balcony. He opened the glass sliding door and stepped outside. Lisa shivered when the cool air brushed her before she stood next to Aaron.

For a couple of minutes, neither of them spoke. They just watched the pleasant view of the lake under the moonlight. Lisa grew impatient with every passing second, but she kept her mouth shut. She wanted to hear from Aaron.

'Do you still have a crush on me?' Aaron gave Lisa a side glance before he added, 'Or did it end in high school?'

'Which one do you prefer?' She wanted to play along with his answer. If Aaron didn't have any feelings towards her, she would laugh it off even if her heart was breaking inside. She would lie that it had been a silly high school crush.

Aaron let out a chuckle. 'I still can't believe you'd have a crush on me.' He shifted to face her before he said, 'But I would like to know the truth.'

'Why?' It scared Lisa to tell him the truth. She didn't want things to become more awkward between them.

'Cause I might share the same feeling.' For a second, Lisa actually believed that she misheard him. Her brain may have been playing tricks on her. But when Aaron took her hand in his, her throat became dry. It wasn't like they hadn't held hands before, but this time it felt different.

'So tell me the truth, Lisa,' Aaron urged.

'Promise me that you will always be my 2 a.m. friend even after I tell you the truth?'

Lisa still remembered her freshman year in college. She was homesick and having a hard time adjusting to her roommate and college. She would call her high school friends every night. As days passed on, all of them got busy. But Aaron would answer her call at any time. He even drove all the way from his college to her campus the very next weekend just to check on her.

Lisa thought she had reached her peak at liking Aaron. But at that time, she hadn't understood how Aaron could make her fall for him deeper whenever he appeared in front of her.

Aaron just smiled at her and squeezed her hand. 'Nothing is going to stop me from being your friend.'

The corner of Lisa's lips curved into a smile before she whispered, 'I have a crush on you every time I see you.'

'So you don't have any feelings when you're not seeing me?' Aaron teased, his eyes twinkling.

Lisa blushed. 'It's not that.'

'Then what is it?'

'Let me finish talking,' she whined, and Aaron chuckled, nodding. 'I always have feelings for you.' Her hazel eyes bored into his green ones. 'It got so hard to suppress them over the past ten years. Sometimes, it felt like my heart would burst if I didn't tell you about my feelings.'

'Why didn't you tell me, then?' Aaron sounded confused.

Lisa grabbed his free hand and held back his hands in a tight grip before she stared at their joined hands. 'Because of this.' She looked back at him. 'I wanted more but was scared that I might lose what we have. When Gwen and Dylan had their first fight during high school, our group didn't eat together for a week. Then you said, "This is what happens when love comes between friendship." I didn't want to lose you in any way.'

'Lisa,' Aaron said, for which she nodded and waited for him to continue, 'I don't even remember saying that.' He groaned, throwing his head back. Aaron met her gaze again. 'I didn't have feelings for you at that time and I only thought you saw me as your friend.'

At this, Lisa's curiosity piqued. 'When did you realise that you have feelings for me?'

Aaron smiled. 'When you left for college, it felt like you had taken a part of me with you.' Lisa stared at him blankly, for which he leaned closer and brushed his nose against hers. 'Why do you think I drove over two thousand miles the very next weekend? I wanted to see you so badly.'

'Aaron,' Lisa breathed out. She waited for a heartbeat before she whispered, 'I'm going to kiss you.'

Aaron's eyes grew a little wide, but Lisa didn't give herself a chance to rethink. She crashed her lips against his. It took a moment for Aaron to realise what was happening, but when he did, he took the lead. Lisa felt Aaron's hunger as their tongues savoured each other's. Her hands roamed over his chest before they looped around his neck. She threaded her fingers into the thick hair at the back of his head. Her lips curled against his in satisfaction.

Aaron pulled back and looked at her, puzzled. 'Why are you smiling?'

Her smile grew wide. 'I always wanted to rake my hands through your brown hair while kissing you.'

Aaron couldn't help but beam at her. 'What else do you want to do with me?'

'Oh! I have a full excel sheet on it.' Hearing Lisa's response, Aaron burst into laughter. But it wasn't just Aaron's laughing she heard; there were more.

'Leave us alone, you creepers!' At Aaron's shout, Charlotte, Dylan, and Gwen stumbled forward from behind a wall. They were laughing like idiots. Suddenly, Lisa felt shy. She wanted to hide in Aaron's arms. Her cheeks flushed when Charlotte gave her a wink.

Dylan kissed his teeth in disappointment. 'Too bad, Lisa. If you had confessed ten years ago, you would have finished that excel sheet by now.' He laughed at his joke. Gwen nudged her elbow into his ribs, making him groan.

Aaron wrapped his arms around Lisa's waist and pulled her closer. 'Don't worry. We have a lifetime to finish it.'

She grinned. 'I know. We can do it slowly.'

Lisa glanced at Dylan and Gwen, who were already poking at each other. She couldn't help but smile. Maybe she might have taken ten years to confess, but she was glad she took the time. It made her experience the real world, her dreams, and her passion for statistics. Aaron had always been next to her in every aspect.

Lisa knew that good partners might not become good friends, but good friends would definitely become good partners. She also knew she and Aaron would live happily.

# 32.

# Connor

Juveriya Bilal

Thirteen-year-old Connor Wolfhard was a considerate and magnanimous teen, trying to cope with the enslaved power of a merciless creature. With the abidance of detest and deep-rooted anger for his contentious mother, he couldn't help but permit himself to be used as an object by the people he was in the custody of Kyle and Riley.

Undergoing all through the difficulties, when all was said and done, the ensuing days embraced his father's return gratifyingly. Surprisingly, the impenetrable visit of the unworldly lost one displayed an unexpected reaction towards his haughty and abrasive older brothers.

Elliot was the only one who didn't give him the cold shoulder, unlike Thibbault and Maverick.

Moving to LA made Connor hope for a little betterment in his life. Oh, just how wrong was he! Maverick and Thibbault didn't leave any stone unturned in bullying him both physically and mentally. On finding him alone, the received feeling was nothing less than a rocket blowing up in the air for him. At least, they could ruffle his feathers as much as they could without any constrictions.

Neither his school life nor his life at home was any good. Besides the three friends he made at school, everybody hated him. Deciding to move to LA meant turning his life into a living hell.

Repeatedly being hurt and harmed by his school bullies didn't affect him much as compared to being a stranger to his own brothers who thought of him so less, exemplary as a punching bag.

However, as the saying goes, 'Nothing lasts forever. When winter passes, spring will return once again.'

The aftermath led him to come across a girl who happened to become a courteously determined resort in his life. Something he never wondered, yet, the sentiments could solely rush in incredulity. Amid being constantly pushed around against the minions in his school.

Her name was Destiny. And perhaps, it was *his* destiny to meet her. She was charming and a classy middle schooler who didn't tend to take shit from anyone. Her remarkable frank personality and shooting candid responses to the students were one of the few things which marked her attraction towards the guys at school.

Although Connor perceived the truth late, until then, she appeared like a knight in shining armour in his life. Protecting him from all the possible obstacles around him. Guiding him in the best way and erasing his insecurities, she did everything she could.

A lot happened in a matter of time. Destiny was his only resort. However, when the pain got too much to handle, being constantly hurt by everyone mentally made him feel that he was a jinx to his family. Wherever he went, the place automatically turned out to be grim.

And Connor ended up doing the worst thing ever in his life.

That was his first suicide attempt.

This wretched and astonishing action didn't only affect his Dad, Elliot, friends, and Destiny, but also Thibbault. As a matter of fact, Maverick was pleased to hear this news. He hated him with every cell of his body.

Sooner, after his recovery, he found a change in Thibbault's attitude.

Thibbault didn't shout at him for anything or made any physical movement to hurt him.

Instead, he began ignoring his existence.

A month later, when Connor went to school, he didn't expect to see Thibbault's car picking him up. Quietly, they both reached home, saying nothing at all through the way.

Little did Connor know that he would receive an apology. A sweetheart like him couldn't stand being displeased with anyone, he wouldn't be able to live the rest of his life willingly with having people regretting or in downs solely because of him.

Although Connor ended up forgiving his older brother, he couldn't forget what he had gone through in the past because of Thibault.

As the good days gradually began opening for him, his father started convincingly making him attend therapy, which consequently felt beneficial to him.

The darkest of dark times started once again when his Mom, Tisha, appeared in their lives, out of the blue.

Resentment, melancholy, betrayal, and abandonment filled Connor's soul throughout. His emotions were all mixed up before he couldn't feel a single thing anymore.

Imagine being abandoned by your biological mother at the beginning of your elementary school and seeing them in the last year of your middle school.

How would you react? Indescribable, right?

Those intense unspoken words he had bottled up all these past years, he tried to let them all out but all he could do was merely stare at her momentarily and shouted even less than a few words, here and there.

The discountenance got the boy nonplussed, briefly.

Although he was unsure of how to react when a word was raised against his father, Connor couldn't be quiet anymore. And him favouring his dad might have been the worst thing, as the result was not only offensive and staggering but completely beyond his wildest dreams.

'What father and brothers are you standing up for? For the father, who was the one to leave you, and for the brothers, who aren't even your real brothers,' his mother shouted.

She let out an inconceivable and deeply hidden truth in front of Connor, once again, not giving any care and attention to the outcoming sentiments of her son.

As a result, Connor locked himself up in his room for a week. Everything felt so confused for him, like a jumbled set of puzzles.

Huge burden. Life appeared like a burden. He wanted to scream, but there was no voice and energy inside him to even do that. He wanted to share his feelings, but he was unable to share anything with anyone.

Nothing felt right for him. His head was spinning, unable to let him think anything straight with activities run on automation. Even his breath felt like a burden at the time.

His loud, voiceful brain had accepted the truth, but his cold heart didn't even want to listen. His pathetic and selfish self missed that week's therapy session, without caring for his father's money.

Dissolving the feelings inside himself, Connor tried his best to cope with his intense emotions. Still, something bothered him. A name, "Melissa," was taken by his mother. He couldn't resist the urge to know her identity. Another month arrived when Connor went to school. Until now, he had had a better life.

A feeling shot up inside him from the thought that his dad did love him, for he wanted to take Connor's custody in the past. In those past years, Connor never had received any kind of love and affection. So, this feeling became overwhelming for him.

After Connor's suicide attempt, both Elliot and Thibbault had become overprotective towards him. So, they rarely let him leave their side. In addition to this, he couldn't even hang out with his friends anymore, because they wouldn't let him leave the house.

If he asked the reason, they would barely say anything. Only Elliot had given him a hint, 'For your safety.'

*What was that supposed to mean?*

Aside from that, Connor had built a great relationship with Destiny.

Although there were good times, he had bad times to experience as well in that time.

Maverick was the one to bribe those middle schooler guys for bullying him unthinkingly so that he would leave LA.

Just like how good feelings took him to cloud nine, the bad feelings would tend to pierce holes through his skull.

How could someone be so heartless? Yes, Maverick wasn't his real brother, still, there was a question raised towards humanity. How could you hate someone for some illogical reason? Jealousy?

As usual, Connor was waiting outside his school in the rain for one of his brothers to pick him up; however, sadly, nobody had arrived until then and shockingly, it was almost 4. Even so, the slight rain has turned into a downpour.

Connor couldn't help but forward his steps to walk home.

While walking, Connor caught sight of the familiar white van passing by his way that he had noticed around the street a few days ago. As he increased his speed, the van veered its direction and drove back. This time, towards his side.

Anxiety struck him. Connor didn't have his bike or anything at all to drive his way home quickly. The only thing he could do was quicken his steps.

Before he could think of anything, he realised he was in the tight hold of the stranger.

He screamed. But nobody listened. In the downpour, people barely could hear voices.

He struggled to lose the tight grasp and eventually, he became successful, too. On his way to running, Connor abruptly came across the person he never wished to see if it was a normal situation.

At the moment, Maverick came out to be a safe place for him. Connor had seen him angry umpteenth times, but this time, he wasn't the reason for his anger. Maverick tried to take his younger brother out of the situation but all in vain. He knew those guys.

They all were the minions of Robin, the brother of the murderer of his mother.

The next moment, Connor realised, the gun was veered in the front direction and as the bang of the gunshot echoed, Maverick fell to the ground.

The last thing he heard was himself wailing out his older brother's name.

As soon as Connor regained consciousness, he found himself locked up in some unknown room. Feelings of tremor drove up and down, all over his body. His face was constricted with terror. The boy couldn't allow himself to move to unlock the door of the room.

At the sound of the click of the door, a mixed-up emotion, filled up with both hope and terror enveloped him. Every time they clicked away, he held his breath.

After a total of eight audible clicks, the door was ultimately unlocked.

Connor couldn't recognise the man who had just appeared in front of him. Though, he had eavesdropped on the name of "Robin" in his father and Thibbault's conversation.

He had a worse feeling telling him that it was actually him.

Robin solely wanted revenge on Jaxon Wolfhard. As Jaxon was the one to put his brother into jail for the cause of his wife's murder, Robin wanted to torture or kill his youngest son since Connor wasn't Melissa's son to take revenge for his brother.

Melissa and Robin's brother had a deep relationship between them; however, Melissa betrayed him in the end and decided to marry Jaxon. Since the man was kind of a psychopath, he ended up murdering his lover in great indignation within a few years.

Now, Robin wanted to do the same to Connor, an innocent boy, who was unworldly and didn't even know about a single event that had taken place in his family's life in the past. It had been long enough since he moved to LA, with his dad and brothers; however, they never mentioned anything in front of him. They tried their best in hiding the news of those unpleasant events from him, because they never wanted him to feel bad when he had already suffered a lot.

Connor never deserved such kinds of things. Then why was it always him?

The moment arrived when Connor found something needle-like being injected into his hand.

Little did he know, it was anaesthesia. Robin wanted to paralyse him so that he could make an effort in selling his kidney as revenge. He was sure of the fact that he could blackmail Jaxon as long as he had Connor under his grasp.

Robin's effort failed eventually. Because the next thing he knew, he was arrested as well.

Once Connor got better, his family let out every single truth to him.

A few days later, Connor caught sight of the letter lying near the entrance door. It wasn't addressed to anybody, merely covered up in a blank white envelope. Unfolding the paper, the powerful words caught Connor's sight.

*Dear child,*

*First and foremost, I want to wish you a happy belated birthday. I wish I was there to celebrate your second teen birthday even if I had missed the first, but the truth is, I couldn't dare to face you. I treated you horribly, and I feel ashamed of my behaviour. You never deserved that kind of behaviour from me.*

*I would try and offer a little explanation for what I did, but there are no excuses. Whether my intentions were good or bad, they don't matter here, only my poor choices and selfish actions.*

*Connor, I gave birth to you. I know I made some unforgettable mistakes, and for that, I sincerely apologise to you. But you should know that I was doing the best I could with what I knew, and with all the pressure and stress enveloping me day by day, everything began spiralling. I truthfully repeat, I never knew about the real self of Kyle and Riley. I thought of them as my friends. Accordingly, I told them about you, and they ended up taking care of you in my absence when I was in the rehabilitation centre.*

*William told me about your abysmal condition. I was appalled. I wanted to come to meet you, but Kyle had got me entangled in the negotiation. I must return his debt, in that only condition he'll let you come with me. How was I supposed to pay off the million dollars I borrowed earlier in the name of great expenses including survival, rent of a house and car, utility bills, and your education? Plus, I had lost my job, though I ended up squandering on drugs and clubs. And the remaining of the arrears were spent on my period of convalescence. I couldn't take it, and there was no point crying over spilt milk.*

*With the help of Evan, William succeeded in reaching out to your Dad. Evan never knew about the rest of our life until I told him. I hope he visited you.*

*I made a lot of blunders, but I never doubted my love for you. If I ever had, I would have sent you with your father on that day.*

*You are so strong and brave. You always have been and will always be. I secretly know that. I wish you the strength to face challenges with confidence along with the wisdom to choose your battles carefully. I may not now carry you in my arms, but I will always carry you in my heart.*

*You have been through a lot because I caused you so much pain, and still, you are standing erect and reading out this letter.*

*You may hate calling me your mother but the proudest and heart-warming moment for me is to call you my son.*

*I'm so proud of you, Connor.*

*With my best regards to Maverick for reaching out this letter to you.*

*Please look after yourself.*

*Love,*
*Tisha*

For the first time, Connor felt so at ease with the world.

The breeze tousled his hair, yet unable to wipe the tiny smile, spread out to his lips as he raised his head to stare at the sky. Everything was in awe of its beauty. His mind relaxed and he felt the happiness of his life bubble up from within.

No, he wasn't happy. He certainly felt happiness.

In a brief moment, he heard a familiar voice originating behind him. 'When I see you, I see myself. You are the junior version of mine.' Connor looked to find his dad, who lightly chuckled, approaching his way. 'You are different from your brothers, Connor. A lot different.'

Staring at Connor with his affectionate eyes, he continued as the boy quietly slid the letter into his pocket. 'Might be real, you haven't got the best parents, but I proudly say, you have proved yourself to be the best son in the world.'

Jaxon stepped forward as a smile of unfeigned delight spread out to his lips. He placed a long and soft kiss on his son's forehead, expressing the profound warmth and tenderness, seeping off him.

It was priceless.

Jaxon ruffled his hair in great affection and walked inside the house, leaving him in intense contentment.

Today was almost still, and Connor was playing in joyful anticipation, absorbing the brilliant shades radiating off nature.

Taking a moment, he determined to feel through himself. The light restrained in his insides began to break out from his pores.

A burst of sunshine sparkled through his soul.

The anguishing tribulation of old doors closed and the new ones of enchantment opened to the future. It was time to start a new and unaccustomed chapter in Connor's life.

33.

# Gone are the Days

Mitali Kushwaha

Gone are the days,
When the first thing of dawn was my mother's voice,
and not the alarm tone.
The only urgency was to maintain the tunic plates,
Watching Dad fill the bottle and Mom wrap the tiffin,
Getting instruction to drink the water
and finish the entire tiffin.
Rubbing polish to make a mirror in the shoe,
When the only complex thing was to tie the lace of the shoe.

Gone are the days,
When the pending work was restricted
to the line written below the homework.
When the longest waiting time was for a week

for games period.

When the strategies were made to eat chocolates,

When the only problem was broken lead pencils.

Sharing nonsense with friends without thinking twice,

When the only pains were of falling,

And punishments were restricted to standing out.

Now I realise the beauty of those days,

When the first sound of the morning is the ear-bleeding tone.

The complexity is of finding life's goal,

And the urgency of getting ahead of all.

Now the pending work makes a paper roll,

All are running to reach an indefinite goal.

The strategies are made to cut costs in no time,

The talks are limited to birthday wishes and valentine.

Business decisions are taken over friendly lunches,

Pain and punishments are in bunches.

34.

## School Love Rhyme

Harleen Kaur

I was a little girl when you came into my life,
every day after I trudged at the edge of a knife.
The first time I saw you smile,
couldn't help but linger around for a while.
We stood by and grew up together,
every year flew by slowly like a feather.

My first crush, my first kiss, my first love,
you kept my heart safe in the clouds above.
You shone for me like light,
everything with you felt just so right.
We ran through hallways,
Our school was our love maze.

Love notes, roses, and football field proposals,
you and I fit with each other like a puzzle.
My eyes on you, yours on mine,
This is our school love rhyme.
After all these years, we and our future is bright,
I promise to be by you—through all kisses and fights.

35.

# Nostalgic Childhood Memories

Dhriti Mehra

Childhood memories, what to apprise about?

Those good-crazy days, and that gimmick love for games.

Those happy-cry full days, and that *katti-abbi* after a fight with friends;

All these things filled our childhood days,

which turned out to be an amazing memorable part of our life.

It doesn't matter,

Whether *katti-abbi* has now become senseless for us,

in those days, it was the sole key to our friendship.

It was as if it was merely a key to the door;

And can you sense for which door?

The door to glee.

Those days when we used to wake up early to go to school,
And the means of transport was our school bus.
That ride to school through the bus was not only to be considered only
as a means of transport for us,
But to be acknowledged as the greatest object in our life.
Watching people out via the window,
Smiling through our hair with our mates,
Was the exciting action that we waited for,
Like we anticipate for a Netflix series to be publicised.

For just a chocolate, countless things were inhabited to perform.
Sometimes, when there was nothing delicious left for us to eat,
The soil was the only source of food for us.
Irrespective of knowing that if we got caught,
We would be punished for such an etiquette.
We enjoyed eating it as much as we could,
by hiding our faces from our parents.

From roaming in Mother's arms, sitting on Father's shoulders,
To smiling and teasing our siblings
Was the best thing to do.
Unknown of what's right or wrong,
Performing every activity we felt like,
To spitting out every single word that our hearts felt
without ascertaining what the conclusions would be,
Was the epitome of sweetness and innocence of our childhood.

That desire of becoming monitor or prefect in class,
Was as if like we are the only king and queen of the domain.
Winning on sports day and coming back home with a pleasant smile on our face,
And receiving a teddy or a beautiful playing doll was the only and most loving gift to us.

That feeling of terror when our siblings used to tell us horror stories,
And not going to the washroom just because inside there lived a ghost.
It was the most usual story of everyone's lifetime.
That craziness to sleep with our parents
was as if we wanted to have a sleepover with our bosom buddy.

# Co-authors
# in this anthology

## Deepika Kumari

A keen writer, artist, observer, and food explorer, Deepika Kumari is an undergraduate student of English Literature. She's a highbrow co-author in various anthologies. Above all, she's a die-hard fan of Rowling's "Harry Potter". On a true note, she's not a bookworm yet, but she's undoubtedly a budding explorer of this mesmerising pen world. Apart from writing, she wants to know "thoda aur" about flavourful stately cuisines, seasoned with love.

## Tiyasa Tikadar

Tiyasa Tikadar is an 18-year-old Wattpad writer, based in West Bengal, India. With a mind of a psychopath, she makes sure to deliver the darkest plot twists to her readers with a dash of romance. She loves to read/write books with dark natures as she believes life is not full of rainbows and hopes to publish her books one day. She also has a soft corner for creepy movies in her heart.

## Mouly Dangarwala

Mouly Dangarwala is an eighteen-year-old engineering student who occasionally enjoys writing poetry. She is an avid reader and is happy to indulge in pretty much every genre that isn't horror. Her poetry book, which she published on Wattpad under a pen name, has also garnered lots of love and made her a part of the wonderful online community of readers and writers.

### Katyani Sharma

Katyani Sharma is an eighteen-year-old who has always had a soft spot for poetry. She's composed many pieces in Hindi, English and Punjabi. With the promise of a bright future ahead, she is pursuing medical sciences and wishes to become a doctor. She is also a hopeless romantic at heart and sees beauty in pretty much everything.

### Rashmita Nayak

Rashmita Nayak has always been passionate about writing narrative poetries. Her debut Wattpad novel "The Last Letter" has reached three lakhs plus readers on Wattpad. After spending most of her life in Nashik, Maharashtra, she is now working as a project coordinator in Mumbai. She has completed her masters in commerce and is now pursuing project Management. Her favourite genres are young adult and romance. Rashmita loves reading and listening to various types of music in her free time.

### Halo C

A believer in absurd dreams, Halo writes in hopes that people may understand that absurdity is logical, as it is what makes humanity a unique and inventive species. When not writing, Halo can be found attempting to rationalise and imagine wild inventions with his friends over a cup of coffee.

## Jasmeen Bagga

Jasmeen Bagga is an eighteen-year-old medical aspirant who has a flair for poetry. She has always been an avid reader; this habit being instilled by her elder sister and her love for books goes beyond her. Her poetry pieces centre on love, loss, and belongingness. She is a supporter of LGBTQ+ rights, and the stories included in this anthology by her revolve around that.

## Ananya Duggal

Ananya is an eighteen-year-old poetess living in the small city of Ludhiana, striking her brush of emotions over pieces of paper. She looks forward to starting her bachelor's degree in psychology. She calls herself a wild rose—a symbol of love and adoration. Her veins sparkle with positivity.

## Sakshi Khillare

Sakshi Khillare is a literature student who wishes to live in a world where we can turn fictional stories into reality just with the flick of a wand. Her love for reading began during the lockdown. She believes that words create a great impact on a person's mind, which is why she's also trying her hand at writing. You can find her socialising on Instagram under her handle @alterrr_e.

## Juveriya Bilal

Juveriya Bilal, a young author, and an enthusiastic epistemophilic who grew up in UP, India, opens up about her fascination for reading as being "addictive" to it, and this interest simply led her to some early exposure to writing at the age of 12. Juveriya generally dabbles in teen fiction which doesn't solely revolve around high-school dramas and relationships but an arresting parallel story as well. As the first lockdown was introduced in India, she stumbled upon her newfound curiosity to write poems. Incredulously, her poem Being Down-Hearted selectively got an opportunity to be published in "Anytime News" of India.

## Namrata Prajapati

Namrata Prajapati is passionate about writing. Her preferred genre is "romance," and she believes words hold the power to mend or break one's heart. Her chaotic mind inspires her to frame words into stories. She is also a content writer and a psoriasis warrior.

## S. R. Behera

S. R. Behera, a Gen-Z writer with liberal ideologies, pens her beautiful thoughts in a mesmerising manner. While pursuing her Master's in literature, she aspires to be a world-class writer.

## Ananya Barman

Ananya Barman is an 18-year-old bibliophile who discovered her passion for writing, reading novels and poetries, which is a form of escape to her own world of imagination. Writing serves as a source of therapy for her. She is looking forward to doing her bachelor's degree in Medicine. She is also a podcaster and runs her podcast named "Between the pages with Ana" on Spotify and Anchor. Her stories can be found on Wattpad under @Ananyaspeaks.

## Arjun Unnikrishnan

Arjun Unnikrishnan is a 17-year-old aspiring poet who enjoys playing and watching football, reading, and writing. He is very jubilant about his participation in this anthology and looks forward to more opportunities like this.

## Yashvi Bulani

Yashvi is an avid reader, writer, speaker, and procrastinator. Along with being a high school student herself, making this anthology a special one for her. She is extremely imaginative while thinking of book ideas and very creatively forgetting about them the next day. You can find her on Wattpad as @pessimistkween and her Instagram is @sass_vi.

**Jash Chauhan**

Jash Chauhan loves writing because it works as therapy for him. Poetry inspires him to scribble his feelings. His poems are a reflection of his soul and his heart. His favourite poet is Rumi, as he relates to the poet's acceptance of situations.

**Krish Malhotra**

Krish Malhotra is a high school student pursuing commerce at the moment, and author of the poem "High School Love". This is his first time getting published, and he is very excited about it. He is a firm believer of fate and hopes to see that it leads him to a bright future.

**Mitali Kushwaha**

Mitali is born and raised in Jabalpur, the humble city of Madhya Pradesh, India. Growing up with a curious mind made her love books from an early age, and being an avid reader helped her express emotions through her writings. She started her journey with poetry when she was 20, and after a short sabbatical (that multitudinous of adult life brings), she is back with her pen again. She mostly writes at night when she is off her motherly duties and spends the day partnering with business leaders to manage the human resource department of an MNC. She is building, mending, and trying to get over every little bit of what life offers, and poetry helps her express it. She pours her heart out at her Instagram @thewordhues and has a world hidden between her pages for all ages.

## Anwesha Banerjee

Anwesha Banerjee is a former teacher who has played with words ever since her childhood. Her bond with writing strengthened during the lockdown and now she aims to traditionally publish a novel which reflects social problems.

## Kriti Mohanty

Kriti Mohanty, an aspiring author and an enthusiastic reader if not already deep into a book, loves to spend her spare time strumming new tunes on her guitar or working on her Bharatnatyam that she has been practising since the age of six. Days to Relive is her first official published work, and she is super proud to present it to every reader looking for some words of wisdom in the form of poetry.

## Kumud Jain

Kumud Jain is an eighteen-year-old student pursuing non-medical and having a keen interest in composing relatable poetry. He is also a huge sports enthusiast, and when not found working hard towards his career of choice, he can be seen binge-watching movies and series.

### Dhruv Kataria

Dhruv Kataria—an overthinker who likes to express his view of the world regarding different topics through beautiful and heart-touching play of words. Dhruv likes to pen poems which describe normal, everyday things but with a different perspective in an emotional yet simple way.

### Huda Nadeem

Huda Nadeem is a teenager living in UAE and figuring out her life day by day. She is an avid reader, a regular fangirl, and enjoys writing poetry as much as cooking and painting. Poetry is what she claims to be her solace, and she hopes that her write-up that's been included in this anthology helps warm people's heart and takes them back to their happy school days.

### Priyanka Reddy

Priyanka Reddy is an ambivert. She loves reading stories, which inspired her to create her own. She tried her hand at writing on online platforms. If Wattpad helped her to grow as a writer, then Radish helped her to become an author. Writing is her passion as well as her career.

## Harleen Kaur

Harleen is currently pursuing her B.Tech in CSE at LPU, Punjab. She's a sucker for cliché Y/A fiction novels. Her love for poetry arose from reading Robert Frost in her high school library for fun. When she isn't reading, journaling, or rewatching her favourite C-dramas, she can be seen vibing to Bieber. Check out more about her at itaintlene.carrd.co

## Dhriti Mehra

Dhriti is a young writer and currently in the lower sixth form. She is compiler of the book named "Eternal Oblivion". Writing poetry is what attracts her in her leisure time. Where she always assumed herself as a poet or novelist in her dreams, today, she is a dog with two tails standing on her feet chasing her dreams fully and purely.

www.ingramcontent.com/pod-product-compliance
Lightning Source LLC
LaVergne TN
LVHW050546160826
845677LV00011B/2201

* 9 7 8 9 3 9 0 8 8 2 7 7 9 *